CO!

SEAL Te........
CONNOR
BY
Jordan Silver
Copyright© 2014 Alison Jordan

Table of Contents

Chapter 1

"I'm here to fuck you."
She watched me from the bed as I
approached her; eyes wide not with
fear as much as with uncertainty. After
all I hadn't given her any indication in
all the months of her teasing and
flirtations that I was the least bit
interested. I kept my feelings well
hidden from her and everyone else
around me. "If you're attached to
whatever that is that you're wearing I
suggest you take it off because it's
going to be in shreds in a second."

She made some sort of noise in
her throat that was cut off when my
mouth came down hard on hers. She
was sweet and soft, just the way I
knew she would be. Which is why I'd
avoided her thus far. A woman like her
has no call being with a man like me.
She's sweet tea and pecan pie on a
southern porch on a hot summer day
I'm pizza and beer. She's cashmere

and pearls in the back of a chauffeur driven limo and I'm leathers and jeans on the back of a chopper. I tried for her sake to leave her alone. No matter how much I wanted to go there I did not want to fuck up her life.

There was no way the people in her circle would ever accept me but she didn't seem to care. From the first time we'd laid eyes on each other she's let it be known through coy smiles and flirtatious laughs that she wanted to be under me. After three long months, hard as fuck months of denying myself and jacking my shit to visions of her first thing in the morning and the last thing at night, I was here to collect.

I didn't give her time to remove the lacy bits of scrap she wore instead I tore it from her body. "Oh…"
"It's okay don't be afraid I promise to take very good care of you. I'm going to turn on this light." I switched on the light next to her bed as she watched my every move. I wanted to see her, all of her.

She had tormented me since the first day I saw her. Her laugh, her smile and her sweet scent have been following me into my dreams. I looked down at her as she rested on her elbow looking at me with hungry eyes. Cool it Connor, if you go at her like you want to you'll scare her half to death, better take it nice and easy this first time. No point in scaring her off before you even got started.

"How did you get in here?" Her sweet southern drawl like something out of an antebellum flick danced over my nerve endings.
"I picked your lock. We have to do something about your door it's for shit. We'll deal with that later." Or there was the other alternative but we'll see how things go. I laid over her on the bed pressing her back into the mattress. I didn't want any more words, tonight was for fucking, branding. There'll be time enough for talking later.

Her breasts were a dream; high and round with pale pink tips that my tongue couldn't wait to taste.

"Umm, fuck I knew you were gonna be sweet." I teased her nipple with soft licks sucking hard one minute, biting down the next. Her body was on fire beneath me and I could feel the softness of her thighs as they opened to accept my weight between them. I was still wearing my jeans and the Henley having only kicked off my boots.

"Undress me." I pushed my hard cock into her soft folds through my jeans as I lifted off far enough for her to pull my shirt over my head. I took her lips again as her hands fumbled with my zipper. Her warm hand wrapped around my length and she sighed around my tongue. I stroked into her hand once, twice. "Too soon." My cock was as hard as it had ever been and I knew that wanting her the way I did, it wouldn't take much for him to blast. I wanted inside of her sweet warmth in the worst way.

Pulling out of her hand I worked my way down her body to her heat. I inhaled her sweet scent first before lapping up her already escaping juices. I fucking knew it. Sweet fucking pussy, her taste went right through me.

What the fuck was I getting myself into here? I was way over my head. This was no one-night stand, not that I ever believed it would be. I'd come here tonight knowing she was going to rope me in, knowing that this one woman was going to be the one. I'd fought it for as long and as hard as I could but in the end it was fate.

"Connor..."She tried pulling my head away. "It's too much." Her body already started to tremble under my tongue. Fuck if she reacted this strongly to my mouth I can't wait to impale her on my cock.

"Ssh, let me have you." I gentled her with my touch, like a stallion with a

mare. Licking deep inside her folds
and teasing her plump clit between my
fingers.

I ate her pussy until my jaw
locked up on me. My cock was hard
and throbbing as I climbed back up her
body. Pushing my jeans all the way off
with my feet I kissed her lips hungrily.
Her soft skin felt amazing under my
hands as they ran all over her. Opening
her legs wider I fingered her sweetness
plunging my fingers deep as she rode
my hand to her third climax of the
night. I meant to bring her off as often
as I could tonight.

We'd both waited a long time
for this and I didn't want to rush it
when I finally got inside her. I wanted
it to last I needed to brand her. The
need was like a living thing inside me.
Something I'd never felt before in my
life, never wanted to. I sank into her as
I looked into her eyes, my hands
caught roughly in her hair. She made a
small sound of distress as I stretched
her with my thickness.

"This is what you wanted take it." I pushed into her sweet as fuck tightness until she'd swallowed all of me. Her pussy was tight, tighter than any I'd ever felt. I had to take a breath and still my movements. The lure of her was almost too much, just as I knew it would be. I stroked into her again and again because I couldn't help it. I had no defenses against her. She'd smashed down my walls. I knew what this meant, what the feelings running through me as I fucked her meant for me, for us. So be it.

"This changes everything Danielle. Do you understand?" She nodded her head yes as she bit her lip, her eyes closed, her pussy locked tight around my cock. I stopped all movement and pulled her head back farther.
"Open your eyes...I need to hear you say you understand me. This changes everything I'm not asking you I'm telling you. You wanted me, I'm here this..." I thrust hard and deep once to

get her full attention. "Says you now belong to me, heart body and soul; you fuck up it's going to be your ass. Do…you…understand?"

"Yes Connor." Her eyes were wide on my face with just a hint of fear this time. I had no doubt I looked like a crazy man on top of her. I could feel the skin drawn tight against my cheekbones the way it did when I went into warrior stance. And this was the hottest battle I'd ever fought in my career.

"I'll give you time to adjust to having a man like me in your life, but heed my warning. The you that you were when you woke up this morning no longer exist. There's no more Danielle. It's now Connor and Danielle. I'll teach you what it means to belong to me later right now I just want to fuck. Are you with me so far?" "Yes Connor please." She curled her pussy up trying to get more of my cock inside her.

That sweet Georgia peach voice of hers is going to get her drilled into the fucking bed time and again. I lifted her legs and spread her so I could fuck her deeper and harder. There was no way I could play the gallant lover, not this first time. Maybe the next round or the one after that but this time was all about me putting my stamp on what I'd finally decided to own. I looked down at where we were joined and her eyes followed mine. She had lost all control of her body.

Gone was the prim and proper southern belle. Beneath me was a woman full of heat and passion. Her nails scored down my back as she fucked up at me trying to get my cock as deep inside her as possible. I gave her what she wanted with a hard pounding thrust that made the bed shake and bang into the wall. Her soft cries were buried in my chest as she licked and bit me there, too far gone to know what she was doing.

That's just the way I wanted her. Her ass moved wildly as her pussy milked my cock. Fuck yeah.
"I love the way you move beneath me, fuck, I always knew you were gonna be trouble. Fuck me."

We tore the sheets from the bed as we rolled over it together. Me on top her on top, me behind her. I fucked sweet Danielle until I had nothing left. It had been a while since I'd fucked. In fact not since the first time I laid eyes on her. Somehow giving what I wanted to give her to someone else seemed wrong. Even when I had no intentions on pursuing her she was all that I'd wanted, all that I'd thought about.

She lay in my arms exhausted from the rigorous fucking. Her skin was red in places where I'd been too rough but she didn't complain. "Sleep sweet Danielle I think I've ridden you enough for one night." She blushed and hid her face in my neck before settling down again. I held her close as her breathing evened out in sleep, and relaxed as I felt my freedom slipping away.

There was no way after having her that anything less than forever would be enough. I'd despaired of ever finding this with anyone. Never gave it much thought after I joined up, but one look at her and the feelings she stirred up inside me were all consuming.

She made me think of happily ever after and family. All the things I'd once sworn would never be for me. I'm just happy that I'd found her now that my life was settled. So that I would never have to leave her behind while I went into battle. I turned our bodies so I could spoon with her for the rest of the night. Until I slipped from her bed at the crack of dawn tired but energized. A night spent in the saddle like that will do that to ya.

"When will I see you again?" She wasn't in much better shape than I was as she laid back against the pillows her body still flushed from that last round of vigorous fucking. I'd grabbed a quick shower in her bathroom to wash away the heavy smell of sex but I still carried her scent on me.

"I have to go to work I'll see you after that. Do you have a lease on this place?" I kept talking as I got dressed to leave. It felt like I was leaving a limb behind or some shit. It's gonna take a while for the newness to wear off I guess. But right now I think I needed at least a year in sweet Danielle before I would be comfortable leaving. "No it belongs to my dad why?" Her soft voice brought me back.
"I just wanted to know how long it would be before you could move."
"Move?"

"Yeah I want you with me. That's a deal breaker. If we do this you're with me" I spoke over her as she was about to say something that I'm sure I didn't want to hear. I'd made up my mind somewhere around the third or fourth time I was fucking her.

We'd crossed the point of no return no point in fucking around now. I've seen enough to know life is too fucking short not to grab it by the balls. And when everything you ever wanted and didn't know you needed fell into your lap you'd be a dumb son of a bitch not to hold on tight. I've been many things in my life dumb has never been one of them.

"But…"
"No buts babe, I asked you if you understood and you said yes. There's no more discussion. Get your shit together I'll be back around six to get you. Stay sweet baby." She knelt in the bed with the sheet wrapped loosely around her as she reached up for my mouth with hers. Rumpled and well fucked that's what she looked like.

"Fuck." I was out of my clothes and between her legs before she knew what hit her. "This is going to be hard and quick baby hold on." I spread her beneath me and with a cursory thrust with my fingers to make sure she wasn't too dry to take me I entered her hard. Her body bucked beneath mine as her legs came up to cradle me. Burying my face in her neck I pounded into her like I hadn't just spent the whole night inside her.

The tight grip of her pussy around my cock had me gritting my teeth against the onslaught of emotions raging through my chest. "How fucking long?" I threw the question out there as it burned through my mind. Her hands clutched at my ass pulling me harder into her heat. I wanted to fuck her all day and never stop, wanted to stay locked inside her until we were both too tired and too spent to draw our next breath.

I found her mouth with mine and ravaged it, biting into her lip as lust threatened to consume me from the inside out. "Never this fucking good." I took her ass in my hands forcing our bodies closer together. I seemed to be trying to draw her into me. To mold us together or some fuck but I couldn't stop myself.

I'd lost all control. All that mattered was this moment and the woman beneath me. The woman I was fucking so hard the bed shook and banged into the wall over and over again. I didn't care as long as she was right there with me and her wild cries coupled with her fingernails digging into my ass told me that she was. "Cum for me Danielle." I latched onto her neck and bit down hard before sucking her skin into my mouth. She screamed and I felt her warm juices flood my cock, that's all I needed to go off inside her hard and long.

We were both out of breath, both panting for air and I couldn't move. She'd done me in, sucked everything out of me. "I knew it, I fucking knew it." I rolled off of her but kept her in my arms. I couldn't even bring myself to let her go, not yet. "Are you mad that we made love again?" I looked down at her question. She seemed a bit confused, as she very well should be. I didn't even know what the fuck was going on and I'd thought I had it all figured out.

"That wasn't love making babe, that was a branding." The question is who the fuck branded who? I pulled her out of bed and headed for the shower. We washed each other in between kisses. Had I ever done this before? Why did she make me want to do sappy shit? What was it about her that made me want to be everything she'd ever wanted? This is bullshit.

"Connor what did you mean…before when we were you know?" She shrugged her shoulders and kept her head down. I pulled her head back with a tight grip in her hair so I could see into her eyes. "Fucking?" She nodded as her face heated up. Fuck me I got myself a shy girl. "Which time?" She fortified herself to look me square in the face as she answered. I could tell it was hard for her, guess she doesn't do too many morning after conversations, which is fucking A ok with yours truly.

"When you growled how long?" Fuck I hadn't even meant to say that shit out loud.
"I meant how long will your pussy own me?" I reached down and pushed two fingers inside the pussy in question making her climb to her toes as her eyes closed. "Fuck Danielle, I can't fuck you all morning I've got shit to do." She bit her lip and nodded but I knew she wasn't hearing me her hips were already moving against my hand.

"Turn and face the wall." I sucked her pussy off my fingers and looked down at my cock, which seemed to have a mind of its own. I've never fucked anyone this much in my life we had to be going for the Guinness book or some shit on this one. "Cock that ass for me baby." I ran my hand down her back to her ass and then switched up. "Change of plans." I knelt behind her and lifted one of her legs for better access. I swiped my tongue the length of her pussy and she twitched. Ooh yeah. I fucked her with my tongue for a good ten minutes from behind with her leg cocked in the air while stroking my hard leaking cock.

I couldn't get enough of her pussy's taste in my mouth and she juiced a lot for her man. When my cock threatened to revolt I stood up and slid into her from behind. Wrapping my arms around her I fucked in and out of her at an easy pace. Work is gonna to have to wait.

This time was sweet and slow, no rush. My cock already knew her inside so I could take my time. The branding was over ownership had been claimed it was now bonding time. "When I get you home I think I'll fuck you for a week solid. I'll let you out of bed long enough to eat but that's it. You think your tight pussy can handle that?" I squeezed her nipples and bit into my new sweet spot on her neck. She was too far-gone to answer but I didn't need one. It is what it is and I plan to fuck her as hard and as often as I could for the next little while.

"Sometimes it will be hard, rough, sweaty and dirty as fuck. Then I'll take you like this. Nice and slow so you know your man can give you both. Now lean over and grab the wall baby." As soon as she was in place my cock went to work, plunging in and out of her like a battering ram. "Fuck yeah, you hear that?"

The slapping sound of our hips meeting was loud and the sweet sound of her pussy juice slipping and sliding all over my dick was the sweetest fucking thing I'd ever heard. Reaching around I pinched her nipples and her ass picked up speed fucking back at me hard and fast. "Connor?"

"Yeah sweetheart right here it's okay, let go I've got you." She flung her head back onto my shoulder and came on my cock with a loud groan. I wasn't too far behind her. Her pussy brought me up to my toes as I tried to dig as deep into her as it was possible to go while emptying my balls inside her with a roar.

We needed another shower and then I really had to go, my brothers were probably wondering where the fuck I was. "Don't make me wait Danielle, be ready when I come for you tonight. Now come kiss your man goodbye and try not to put too much sweet in it I need to get the fuck gone." She walked over to me holding her towel together.

I took her in my arms and kissed her cute as fuck nose. "Stay sweet baby I'll see you later." I didn't dare risk kissing her the way I wanted to again, who knows when the fuck I'd come up for air. I kissed her quick but she turned her face up for more. "I'm not sure that's a good idea babe." She pouted at me. "So fucking cute." I gave her what she wanted and then with a finger trailed down her cheek I left.

Chapter 2

Back at the compound where I lived with the men I considered my brothers I got ready for the day. I was getting a bit of a late start which none of the nosy fucks let me forget as they tried sticking their noses in my business as soon as I caught up with them. I was prepared for their shit, which I knew would be forthcoming. I'm the one always saying this relationship shit wasn't for me. I wasn't against it for others but it just wasn't for me.

Now I would be the first to take the plunge. I wonder if I should let them in on just what the fuck was in store for them when their time came? This all-consuming obsession that fucking ties you up in knots and owns your ass. I think I've become part bitch overnight or some shit. What the fuck am I thinking?

"Fuck Connor you smell like a bitch."

"Fuck you Zak." I smacked him behind the head as I went by on my way to the coffee. The other five assholes were all staring at me like I was some sort of anomaly.

"Fuck bro I know that scent." Logan sniffed the air around me. He better not know that fucking scent.

"What the fuck! you assholes don't have anything better to do? We suddenly cleaned up the streets and we're having an off day?"

"Whose scent is it Logan?"

"I can't put my finger on it Quinn but I know it." He looked like he was really giving it some serious thought. If anyone could sniff out what's going on it would be my brothers in arms. Seven ex SEALs who'd spent the last ten years together both on duty and off.

We were closer than most brothers of blood. Just this once though I wish they would mind their own damn business. I wasn't quite ready to share yet. I wanted to savor the newness of it first before life intruded. I sound like a bitch.

"If you're through sniffing my ass maybe you girls want to fill me in on how things went last night?" Anything to get the meddling fucks off the scent.
Everyone grew serious because what was going on in our little burgh was no laughing matter. Some fuck was using our backyard to traffic drugs and what we suspected might be worse or so it seemed. So far we haven't been able to find anything but suspicions were high.

Our little town in Georgia was a perfect little out of the way haven. Its close proximity to the water and underground caves along with some other shit that we had yet to explore made it the perfect venue for criminals of a certain ilk. We knew from experience that these were the perfect breeding grounds for some serious shit. Out of the way, not really on anyone's radar. It was the ideal spot to carry out all manner of criminal activities.

We'd scoped out the area first thing to make sure we had our flanks covered from all angles. Yeah it was a bit over the top bordering on paranoid but we believed in better safe than sorry. There hadn't been any red flags but that had been almost two and a half years ago. Though we'd seen the potential for some shit if someone was of the mind to go that route.

It would appear some enterprising soul had reached that same conclusion and was now making good on it. What they didn't know was that there were now seven ex SEALs taking up residence here who were not about to let that shit happen. We've only been here less than a year. None of us had ever lived in this town before so we were new to the area. No one knew who the fuck we were and of course seven grown men descending on them out of nowhere must've been food for the fodder.

There were whispers and speculation of course but since we never answered any questions other than our names the town's people had learned not to ask. What conclusions they'd drawn on their own was anyone's guess, but we weren't really interested in that shit either. We just wanted to get settled in and do our thing while being left the fuck alone.

Bikes and tats put fear in people but if someone wanted to pass judgment without having all the facts that was on them. So far no one had approached us with any bullshit and we hoped to keep it that way. The way I see it, we didn't go around asking people who the fuck they were so they should give us the same courtesy. This was home now, one we planned to make ours and we'll fit in in our own way the way we always did.

We'd all grown up in different parts of the country but our old commander had been from right here born and raised. When he'd died three years ago. For some fucked up reason he'd left this land and all his earthly possessions to the seven of us. It had made our decision when the time came for early retirement that much easier. As members of the same team we'd each put in a few more years of service, but we'd all known from day one that we were going to not only keep the land, but we were also going to make this town our home.

Not really having any ties to any one place it was easy for us to make that decision. After years of eating, sleeping and fighting together we knew each other inside and out and trusted one another to have each other's backs. So it only made sense that we would stay close to each other when we came back to civilian life.

Two years ago we'd drawn up plans for what we wanted to do. The one thing we all knew for certain was that we wanted to stay together. There was more than enough land for the houses we wanted to build. The first thing we'd done was build up a high wall around the perimeter so no one knew what was going on inside.

The town's people thought it was some new development going up but we'd cordoned it off to start construction on the homes we were going to have built; and since we were still on active duty then we didn't want to leave the place unprotected. Not the most trusting motherfuckers I know but we trusted no one except each other.

Construction had been started six months later with each of us getting two acres. We situated our homes in such a way that they were literally right next door to each other. The land was in the back and to the front but. Off a ways from the houses we'd built our office. It's where we were planning to run our construction firm.

We'd decided a long time ago even before our commander had been so generous, that when we left the service this is what we would most likely be interested in. We could easily have gone into security or something of the like but after years spent securing land air and sea we pretty much wanted out.

The houses were done in a year and a half. We couldn't do everything ourselves because of our duties but we'd worked on each other's places when we had down time and that had sped up the process quite a bit. Six months after we'd settled in and hung out our shingle so to speak, we'd caught wind of the shit that was going on around us.

There's no way in hell we're going to let shit like that take root in our backyard. After years of fighting and danger the name of the game was peace and quiet. Now for me that shit had been amped up a notch. I have a woman to protect. I don't want this shit anywhere near her so the sooner we got to the bottom of whatever this was the better.

The town's people after realizing that we weren't here to start shit had pretty much accepted us with open arms. Well most of them had anyway and as far as they knew we were navy men. No one knew what faction we'd been working for as that shit tended to be top secret for good reason. Most of them probably still thought we were a biker gang, which we weren't. We just loved to ride. I could understand how seven rough looking fuckers all over six feet tall with tats might give them that idea but we were on some other shit.

Though we were in the midst of a recession. With our connections and the Commander's which he'd hooked us up with through papers he'd left behind, we already had some sweet jobs lined up to do construction on government buildings among other things. If things kept up and the government didn't fuck up the economy anymore than it already had we stood to stay in the black for a long time to come.

These days we did a whole other kind of demolition and I don't think any of us missed the other. War is hell. Now with this new development we were spending our nights doing recon and shit. I guess old habits died hard.

Whoever was behind it was proving to be a wily fuck though because so far we had nothing. It wasn't easy for seven men on bikes riding the streets at night to be conspicuous, especially in a town where the biggest action was bingo night at the lodge. Everyone wanted to know everything all the time.

Those who'd accepted us were mostly part of the older crowd who'd known the commander and they mostly wanted to talk about our navy days. Which was usually a short conversation unless we made shit up. We couldn't share the shit we'd done with anyone, but the old guys still liked hanging around us. We'd started hanging out at the local bar to keep our ears and eyes open but so far we hadn't seen any unknowns coming and going which led us to believe it was a local doing this shit.

"So did we find anything last night or not?"

"We think we're closing in on a few hot spots but right now the fuckers are proving to be a little slippery." Logan passed me a plate of eggs and bacon. For now since there were no women in our mix we all tended to gather at one house for meals. Today was Logan's turn for breakfast duty.

I guess to some it might seem strange for seven grown men to be this close. We pretty much did everything together. But after spending so many years together in some of the most fucked up situations imaginable we were comfortable with each other. We ate meals together we hung out together; it was very rare to find one of us alone without the others. We'll never outgrow that pack mentality I guess. I don't think any of us would know how to be any other way at this late stage in the game. We were in it for life.

This whole business with the trafficking thing was a bother that none of us wanted to deal with. We were all just looking to settle down and enjoy the fruits of our labor away from the fuckery. The old guy who'd first come to us with his suspicions didn't have too much information but he had enough to peak our interest. An old pal of the commander's, he knew a little more about who we were than the rest of the town so he knew we would want to know about that kind of action in our own backyard.

We'd cautioned him to stay quiet about the things he'd shared with us because we had no idea who or what we were dealing with yet. These characters didn't take too kindly to folks sticking their nose in their shit. And in our experience you could never be too careful. Sometimes the least likely suspect turned out to be the guilty party.

Him and a few of his friends who hung out down at the lodge swears there's some kind of gang activity afoot. Strange men in and out of town in the last few months and lots of foot action down on the old boardwalk after dark. He'd reported some type of vessel coming and going at strange hours every few weeks or so. It all spelt trouble to us but we tried to play it down so as not to scare the old guys half to death.

They all fashioned themselves as PIs or some shit. So to keep them from getting caught up in something that might get them hurt or worse we'd promised to look into things. I'm not sure they'd heed us about keeping their noses out of it though. These men were die-hard patriots who had lots of pride in their little burgh where most of them had spent their entire lives.

I could see why they loved the place so much. It was quaint and still full of old world charm. The old homes here were as old as the city;

those old antebellum structures that conjured up visions of lawn parties and ladies in period dress. That's how I see Danielle. That old world genteel beauty and grace seemed ingrained in her.

"Huh, the old guy said he thought they were using the old boardwalk; anything show up there yet?"
"Nope, we checked over every part of that place and there was nothing. We do have that list though and we're still working down the line we'll get something. So you wanna tell your brothers why you smell like roses?" Logan grinned as the others chimed in.

"Connor you got laid?" Zak is such an ass; my glare didn't keep his big mouth shut. They all kept trying to figure it out.
"You fucks wanna mind your own damn business?" Damn it's like we were in a hole in the desert playing the waiting game. Waiting to blow some fuck's head off his body for being

stupid and there was nothing to do but talk shit to and about each other to kill time. I sniffed myself to see just how strong her scent was on me. Fuck.

"Danielle Dupre." Logan snapped the front legs of the chair he'd been leaning back in back into place with a thud.
"Fuck Logan." I gave him a hard glare. How the fuck did he sniff that shit out? I calmed a little when I remembered that that's how she'd first caught me. It was her scent that had brought her under my radar. After that it hadn't been hard for the rest of her to reel my ass in.

"Thought you weren't gonna go there brother?"
"Is there a problem Ty?"
"Nope, just saying. We had this long drawn out conversation where I told you to go for it and I distinctly remember you giving me a laundry list of reasons why that wasn't such a good idea."
"Yeah well shit changed."

"Congratulations man. So when are you bringing her home?" Logan was grinning like a proud papa the ass.

"Tonight."

"You need help with the move?"

"Nah my place is already furnished if she wants to change shit she can just buy what she needs."

"She knows she's moving in here?" Quinn asked while refilling my coffee, nosy fuck.

"Yep." That got a good laugh out of all of them but I just gave them the finger. They pretty much knew that I'd most likely ordered her as opposed to asking her.

"Let's go slackers that building isn't gonna erect itself." I pushed back from the table and got to my feet.

"We were waiting for you lover boy. You sure you got enough strength left for this?"

"Piss off Quinn." We headed out for work some in trucks some on bikes. I had to leave my bike home since I would be picking up my woman and her shit after work. My woman, fuck that felt good.

Chapter 3

We each had our part to play when it came to the business. As equal partners in a business this size and being who we are. Men who don't trust anyone outside our core, we had to handle everything ourselves. We had a secretary to field phone calls because none of us wanted to do that shit but everything else we handled ourselves.

No accountants no lawyers none of that shit. Everything was done as a team, all decisions had to be approved by all or it was a no go. So far we hadn't had any problems and weren't expecting any. We'd protected each other in some of the worst the world had to throw at us I saw no reason we couldn't do this just as well. That's what comes from having each other's best interest at heart. I never thought I'd feel that way about anyone else but my brothers. Never thought I could let anyone else get that close. Fucking Dani had done it with ease.

I didn't even mourn my freedom. I didn't feel constricted the way I always thought I would. Quite the opposite, I actually felt freer somehow. Weird fucking feeling to be looking forward to losing your freedom, this falling in love shit is a racket and women are slick as shit. All sweet smiles and come and get it looks. Leading you around by your dick. That wasn't so bad I guess, but when they wrapped themselves around your heart that's when your ass was in trouble. Shit.

We each agreed that the reason the commander had left his earthly goods to us was because he'd overheard us on plenty occasions talking about what we wanted to do when we got out. The one thing we wanted was to stay together. There was no question of that and we had two choices of what kind of business we wanted to have, security or construction.

To a man we chose construction. After living a life of uncertainty it was good when things just fell into place like they have been since we came back stateside. And our new home wasn't too shabby either. It was a far cry from what any of us had known before.

The town had about twelve thousand residents most of whom had lived her their whole lives. Not exactly a metropolis but Savannah wasn't too far away maybe forty-five minutes if we felt the need for a big city getaway.

Business was looking good so far and we were slated for jobs as far away as Atlanta and even into the Carolinas.

We weren't strapped for cash. The SEALs paid pretty well and it was a good living. Especially for men who didn't have families and knew from early on what they wanted to do with their lives when they got out. The commander had also hooked us up with a good money guy after he started taking an interest in us outside of navy life.

Coming from money himself, he knew a lot of the ins and outs of that world. A world seven young guys who at the time of their meeting were from some of the worse neighborhoods in the country knew fuck all about.

He'd handpicked us right out of combat training to form the special team. We were like a force within a force, not even the navy knew what the fuck we were doing half the time. Not only had he overseen our Ops, but he'd also taken a personal interest and that's how we ended up where we are now.

It was hugely due to him and his talks that we had found ourselves on the paths we'd taken in life. I guess you can say the old man had molded us into the men we are today. Men who could be proud not only of their service to their nation, but also of who they were inside as men.

I knew for myself I'd come a long way from the hell that had been my beginnings. I didn't even want to think about that shit today. I wanted nothing to blacken my day. I'd just made a monumental change in my life. She was the best part of me, the best thing to ever come into my soiled world. Fucking amazing.

We rode through town to the jobsite no doubt looking like a caravan of thugs. I'm pretty sure this town had never been overrun by the noise of six Harleys at top speed. I never really gave two fucks what anyone thought of me, or my brothers before; but I'm guessing shacking up with Dani might change that. I played around with the thought in my head for a hot minute. Nah, not gonna happen. I still don't give a fuck. She knew what I was when she started making eyes at me. She'll deal.

We pulled into the lot where the rest of our crew was already hard at work. Our present project is an office complex that if done right would take us at least half a year from start to finish to complete and we planned on doing it right. We charged top dollar for anything we signed on for because we had other men and women to support.

Men and women that the government had fucked over after

they'd lost part of themselves fighting a war not of their making. We already had a waiting list a mile long of more of our brothers and sisters looking for work. This little town was gonna be overrun with old seadogs by the time we were through because we didn't plan on leaving anyone behind.

"Hey Rosie you sure you wanna get all sweaty and shit? Might take away your girl's scent brother."
"Fuck off Quinn. They all had a god laugh at that before we got ready to do our thing.

We put aside all the bullshit as we got to work. The foundation had already been laid and the outer walls built up with reinforced steel. Logan had made the call to go back to the old way of doing things. It cost a lot more but once we explained things to the owners they were more than willing to fork over the money.

This area was prone to hurricanes and a rogue tornado or two over the last decade. When other matchstick buildings would blow in the wind we were building this one to last. We were building the first thing to be erected in Briarwood since the fifties or some shit so there was a lot of interest from the town's folk.

There was a new business whose headquarters were in Atlanta but it was cheaper for them to have offices here since Real Estate prices were insane these days.

The head guy is some type of oil tycoon or some shit with offices all over the south and Midwest. He's already making noises about hiring us to do some other jobs for him because he likes our shit. At this rate we'll be in the black for a while yet, which for a new business is always a good thing. But for the shit we want to do it's excellent.

I thought of her pretty much every other minute throughout the day. Which was fucked because I could seriously lose a limb if I wasn't paying attention. I can't believe she's mine, fuck. It's like my birthday and Xmas rolled into one. I felt like smiling all the damn time for no fucking reason whatsoever. The fuck?

The first time I ever laid eyes on Dani she was with our office manager Candy. The two women were good friends though Candy was from the complete other end of the spectrum from my girl. Dani is old southern money. Her family owns half of the fucking state while Candy's ancestors were coal miners. That's another thing I like about my girl, she doesn't put on ears like some of the other fucks around here.

We'd thrown a little party for Candy's birthday and Dani had been one of her guests. One look and I'd felt my heart hurt. That alone had convinced me to stay the fuck out of her way. I didn't like that feeling of lost control, or the way my eyes couldn't seem to help seeking her out throughout the night. Everything about this fucking woman had teased my senses. Her walk her laugh; every little thing she did. Even the way she flung her hair over her shoulders to get it out of the way.

I'd noticed her noticing me too and that hadn't made shit any easier. My dick was hard for damn near three hours that first night. And when some guy at the bar had hit on her I'd wanted to plant my fist in his face. I've never reacted that way to any woman before in my life.

Living the lifestyle I'd lived in the service I never thought it was fair to subject a woman to that shit. Never know when you might be called up or some shit. Plus I'd heard horror stories of affairs and shit and knowing me I'd probably end up doing twenty five to life so I'd steered clear. Was lucky enough to keep myself protected. I fucked when I needed to but I kept my heart out of the fucking equation.

But that night she'd followed me with her eyes as much as I was trying to pretend that I wasn't doing the same. She stood out like a jewel in a tarnished crown in her designer blouse and her silk skirt with those heels that made her legs look like sin. It had been hard as fuck ignoring the invitation in her eyes. The hunger that I saw there, but I'd done it.

I'd done it every other time our paths had crossed too; until yesterday when she'd walked by me on the sidewalk and acted like she didn't see me. I guess she'd grown tired of me ignoring her and decided to give me a taste of my own medicine. But that shit hadn't sat well with me at all. I guess you can say that was my wake up call. She'd let it be known in little ways that she was interested but I'd avoided her. Until last night!

Now she's mine and there's no going back. That shit scares the fuck out of me. I'm not the settling down type, never wanted to be. I know what I come from, the legacy the two fucks that had spawned me had passed down, and I never wanted to continue that cycle. But now here she was and everything she is forced me to put aside my prejudices against anything domestic and just go full tilt.

My brothers always joked that it would take a very special kind of woman to bring me to my knees. I guess they were right after all. Everything about her just does it for me. From her sweet as honey voice that just makes me want to fuck her into the wall every time I hear it. Her laugh that reminds me of tinkling bells, and the sweetest smile.

And I haven't even started on her kickass body; not too tall at about five foot four, she's a good foot shorter than my six four frame, small and petite. She's the beauty to my beast.

She has dark hair and green eyes to my blonde and blue and everything about her just sings to the man in me.

There's still a lot I didn't know about her though, things we'll have to talk about. I had no doubt that she will catch hell from family and friends for her choice in a mate but that was too fucking bad. I'd made a promise when I was buried deep in her last night into the morning, a promise that I aim to keep.

I hope she was ready for what she'd unleashed. There were things I wanted from her that I'm not sure a girl like her would even know about. My body hardened just thinking about all the ways I wanted to love her and be loved by her. I know with a woman like that I'll have to be on top of my game.

Thankfully I'm in a position to keep her in the style she was accustomed to. But even had I not been she would've had to learn to deal.

What I wanted from her was a forever kind of deal. One man one woman for all time. She's the only one to ever bring that out of me, and I'm pretty sure lightning doesn't strike twice so this was it. For both of us.

Chapter 4

My day couldn't end fast enough.
I was in a hurry to get back to her, to
move her out of her place and into
mine. To have her where I can protect
her. To some it may seem like I'm
moving fast, well except my brothers.
They'd understand the need for me to
do things this way. And I didn't really
give a fuck what others thought,
especially not when it comes to my
woman.

I have one way of doing this shit.
All the way or not at all, and after
being buried in Danielle's sweet pussy
all night I knew it was going to be all
the way. In fact from the first glide of
my dick inside her I knew she owned
my ass. So there's only one thing left
to do. Tie that shit down quick.

I'd put my stamp on her last
night, having her set up in my home
will just seal the deal. I'll spend the
next few weeks getting to know her

and letting her get to know the man she'll be spending the rest of her life with. I think that's only fair since I plan on consuming her life completely from now on and there was still a lot we didn't know about each other.

I know she works running a charity with her mom but that's about all I know about her work. I know she dresses like she's walking off the pages of a fashion magazine and she smells like heaven. I also know she makes me hard just thinking about her and there's no way I'm ever going to let her go especially not after having her.

She was in my blood now, I hope like fuck she could deal with my shit. She'd made a good start last night. No matter what I threw at her she'd taken me and I'd had a lot of fucking to do. After weeks of wanting and denying myself I'd made a meal out of the poor girl. I have no doubt she'd be sore today but maybe tonight I can eat her

CONNOR SEAL TEAM SEVEN | 57

little pussy and make it all better. Fuck there goes my dick.

"Bro you've got the biggest fucking grin on your face." Logan's voice carried across the construction yard to me so of course the other ladies heard and had to give their two cents. "Maybe we should give him the day off, he's been staring at that two by four for the last ten minutes like he's forgotten what it's for." Ty went back to spackling the wall he was working on and I ignored his ass. "I thought he was gonna kiss it there for a minute he was staring at it all lustful like." I gave Cord the finger and went back to what I'd been doing. They were right though I'd gotten lost in my head.

Shit if she was gonna affect me like this I'm gonna have to figure something out. Maybe after a couple weeks of constant fucking I can get back to normal and she wouldn't consume my every thought as she was now. I knew it would be like this, knew she'd take over my fucking life, a little bitty thing like her making a grown man sweat.

She was waiting for me when I got there later that evening. I'd barely given myself enough time to get cleaned up at the site before going to get her. I couldn't wait to bring her home with me, to have her where I can get to her at will. Not only to fuck her, but to protect her too.

Always foremost in my mind was keeping her safe. For a man like me having seen the shit the world has to offer, finding something like this, so rare to begin with. It makes you crazy thinking of ways to protect and shield. More than any nation or any high profile dignitary that needed protection, she was now my number one concern. Any fucker that even looked at her wrong was in danger.

"You ready?" I could tell that she was a little nervous but she nodded all the same and started picking up her bags.

"Leave them I'll get them." She smiled shyly at me as I walked over and wrapped her up in my arms kissing her long and hard.

"Umm, I needed that. You missed me?"

"Like crazy." She cuddled into my chest where my heart was beating out of control. It does that whenever she's anywhere near; that and my dick gets iron hard. I wanted to fuck but I wanted her home even more so I had to calm my dick the fuck down.

"You scared?"

"A little, I've never done this before."

"There's nothing to be afraid of. I told you I'd take care of you didn't I?" I looked down at her inhaling the sight of her. All I wanted to do was drag her over to the bed and fuck her into forever. But I wanted her in my bed in my home under me the next time I took her, that shit was important to me.

"Yes but shouldn't we date each other first?" She laughed shyly up at me and I couldn't resist kissing her cute little nose and her brows. "Isn't that what we've been doing the last few months? All that flirting and those coy looks of yours? I thought that was our mating dance. It doesn't matter we're beyond that shit now let's go."

I took her stuff down in four trips. My girl had lots of clothes as was to be expected; but damn how much shit do women collect? It's a good thing I had room in the truck and a rack on top. "Did you want to take any of this furniture with you?" If she did we'd have to rent a truck or some shit over the weekend. "Maybe my writing table." She pointed out a piece of furniture that looked like something you'd see in a museum.

"How old is that thing?"
"It was my great great grandmother's, late seventeen hundreds I think."
Damn shit was probably worth more than my house.
"Let me help you that's heavy."
"No way Dani out of the way."

I got her settled in my truck with the desk strapped to the top and we headed for the compound, where I'd had to threaten the guys to stay hidden at least for tonight. They were all chomping at the bit to meet her officially. She would be their first sister in law so I had no worries that they would all be welcoming. I just didn't want her to be overwhelmed her first night in her new home and nothing is more overwhelming than a team of nosy as fuck ex SEALs.

She seemed to relax as we drove and I learned a little something about her; my girl is the touchy feely type. She held my hand while I drove and fuck if I didn't like that shit. Her hand was so soft and small in mine that I felt my heart clutch. Please let me do this shit right.

One of the reasons that I'd fought the attraction so hard was that I never wanted to see sadness on her beautiful face. It would kill me to fuck up her life in anyway. I just didn't see how someone like her could ever be with someone like me. Now after the night we'd shared, I cant see it any other way.

"You ever been on the back of a bike baby?" I kissed her knuckles because shit, I couldn't help myself. Even in jeans and a soft T-shirt she was hot as fuck. Her tits pushed against the material making two indentations and I knew she was turned on because her nipples were hard. It took all my concentration to stay the course and not pull over and take them into my mouth. I moved her hand to my dick, which was now trying to tear through my jeans it was so fucking hard. She blushed of course but kept it there.

"No I've never been on one before. It's looks fun but scary at the same time. I do love to watch you guys when you're riding out together though, I think it's sexy."
"You do do you? What would you say if I told you you would be the first woman to ever get on one of those bikes?"

"Really? Wow, why is that?" I doubt she realized her fingers were squeezing my cock and then rubbing it out. I couldn't help pushing into her hand for more. Should I let her in on just how much power she now had over me?

There was a reason for us not letting just anyone on the back of our bikes. Like our homes that shit was sacred, yeah we're fucked up like that. There had been a great many who'd wanted the privilege but had been shot down. A fuck was a fuck but the keeper was a whole different story. A man's bike was for his keeper.

"Only a man's true mate should ever be on the back of his bike. I think our rapping brothers call it a ride or die bitch."
"Um, I'm not hip what exactly does that mean?"
"It means that if shit gets real I trust you to be there with me one hundred percent. It means through thick and thin. All the things marriage used to mean but have since fallen the fuck off. You getting this?"

"I think so but…"
"Don't sweat it right now babe. We'll go over all that shit at a later date. Just know for now that you're the only one I've ever even considered having there and that means a lot to me. It also means a huge change for you. You do realize that I'm never letting you go ever right?"

I didn't bother looking over at her to see if she accepted my dictate or not. That ship had fucking sailed when she wrapped that sweet as fuck pussy around me and sucked my life essence the fuck out of me. A man knows when he's cumming just to break one off and when he's planting seeds in a garden he wants to grow. Little Danielle's gonna find herself bred before the fucking year was out. I have no doubt. Fucking game changer.

Chapter 5

The boys were nowhere to be seen when we pulled in but I was sure the nosy fucks had us within their sights. She looked around in surprise, which was understandable. Not too many people knew what existed behind these walls. We'd built them that way purposely; our own little haven away from everything and everyone else. It just made people more curious but that was easier to deal with than being out in the open feeling exposed.

It was going to be fun to see how I did living with someone else. Pretty sure it was gonna take some getting used to. She wasn't anything like my brothers I might have to brush up on my etiquette and shit. I got out and helped her out of the truck before getting started on her million and one bags.

"Welcome home Danielle." I hugged her loosely around her middle and stole a kiss before setting her aside. Nosy fuckers were probably snickering behind windows and shit. If any of them came out here I'll flatten the fucker.

"This is beautiful Connor, Candy told me a little about the place but not much. I think she signed a privacy clause or something." She laughed a tad uneasily.
"Close enough." I lifted a couple of her bags from the truck and headed for the house before I realized that she wasn't falling in step next to me. I looked over my shoulder to find her just standing there. She looked at me in surprise. "I was kidding."
"I wasn't come on let's go before they come out here."

She searched my eyes to see if I was playing around but the truth is that her friend had had to sign something that we'd come up with to protect our privacy; we took that shit very seriously.

We've all been in some situations before that if certain people were to ever discover our identities there could be trouble. That's one of the reasons for us sticking together like this, the reason we all knew we will be spending the rest of our lives together. It had been a stroke of luck that the commander had left us this land. We would've found another place somewhere else no doubt, but this was as good as any. Plus it had saved us a fuck load of money.

"Connor I really was kidding you…"
"I know; did you eat?" I didn't want her getting scared so I needed her to drop it. The truth is we're a clannish secretive bunch and she was now part of that shit. She'll get used to it eventually.
"No I wasn't sure what you wanted to do." She was so fucking quiet and

reserved. What the hell did she see in me anyway? Fuck if I know.

"You want to go out to eat or you want to make something here?" We were finally inside and I only had a few more bags and her desk to grab. "I'd love to make something here." "Sounds good let me grab the rest of your stuff and I'll show you around okay sweetheart?" I couldn't resist stealing another kiss on my way out the door. So fucking sweet.

I showed her around the house after dropping her stuff off in our room. Our room, yeah I like the sound of that.

"This is all very beautiful Connor." We were standing in the middle of the sunken living room with the fireplace that was almost as tall as she was. I'd put a lot of effort into this place. At the time I had no idea someone like her would be gracing it with their presence. I'm glad now that I'd gone the extra mile.

"Yeah well it's home now so you can feel free to change anything you want. I'll set up an account for you for anything you want to do with the house. Tomorrow we'll go down to the bank and get your name on my accounts…"

"Connor don't you think that's a bit much? I'm sure you know I have money of my own I don't need to take your money."

I studied her for a long time without saying anything. How can I put this so she doesn't run out the door screaming before she'd even got settled in? And what the fuck had happened to men that women thought they had to take care of themselves even after they were under a man? A real man was supposed to take care of that shit. If she was a feminist I was about to fuck her whole program up royally because I don't play that shit. My woman's my fucking responsibility and fuck anyone who doesn't agree. The fuck!

"I take care of you from now on Danielle no debate on that. I don't care what you do with your money but anything to do with the house is on me. Your clothes and shit are on me, though you may put me in the poor house." I tried to lighten the mood because I didn't want this to turn into a thing and from what little I'd seen so far she could be a little stubborn. I didn't want that to change. She could be as stubborn as she wants with others but when it came to this, to us. I rule this shit no question.

"I don't know about that Connor."
"Don't argue with me Danielle it won't work, just do as I say and we'll be fine. Let's go find something to eat." The sooner she learned that I'm not the arguing kind the better. I grew up with that shit and I'd be fucked if I'm gonna have that in my life. As far as I'm concerned there's only one way for a relationship to work. As the man it's my responsibility to love, cherish and protect. Anything that stands in the way of that is dead. It's also my place as her man to take care of her in all things and the moment she accepted me into her body for the first time she gave me that right.

She followed me into the large open-air kitchen where we scrounged around for something to cook.
"We have the makings for pasta Alfredo, salmon filets; we can fire up

the grill but I'm afraid that might be a red flag to my brothers to haul ass over here."

"I don't mind." She looked over my bent shoulder into the refrigerator as I tried to find something good for our first meal together.
"I do, I want you all to myself for tonight. So what's it gonna be? I forgot to ask you're not like a vegetarian or anything are you? I never once saw you eating."
"I eat pretty much anything as long as it's dead."
"Are there live things you can eat?"

We joked and teased each other as we prepared a light meal of pasta with garlic bread and a salad. We moved smoothly together, like a well-coordinated dance routine. Every once in a while I stole a kiss or copped a feel. But I liked it best when she was the one stealing kisses and touches of her own with no prompting from me.

It felt right having her here, sitting across from her having a light conversation over a dinner that we'd prepared together, our first of many. She was my fucking reward. After a life of bullshit this amazing creature was my prize. I could do that shit all over again if I knew it would lead to this.

Fuck she owns me. How the fuck did that happen, and so effortlessly too? Just a look and a smile and she'd hooked me. Shit was more dangerous than flying mortar. I have to admit that even though I've been in some tight spots before where my life was threatened. I don't think any of them scared me as much as sitting here at this table looking at everything I always wanted and never knew I did; and praying not to fuck it up.

After dinner we cleaned up together and then had coffee. There was something plaguing me as we sat there. Something that I'd never asked another woman in my life. Never cared truth be known but with her I needed to know.

"We need to talk but we're not doing it in here, let's step outside." She followed me out the door to the backyard. Standing in front of her it hit home just how small she really was compared to me. Last night when I'd been fucking her, her small stature had been the last thing on my mind.

Now looking down at her so tiny and fragile looking it hit home for the first time what it really meant to have a woman that you wanted for your own. How much more vulnerable she seemed. How can I protect her always? Did all men have these questions? I'll have to take that out and look at it later. There was no point in asking one of the others because they'd never been here before either, I'm the first to wade into these waters.

"Who had you?"
"What?" She took a step back. I could see that my question had thrown her but I wasn't about to let up. I needed to know.
"Last night when I took you, you weren't a virgin. Not that I expected it of a twenty five year old woman but I need to know." Just saying that shit fucked with my head. It was completely irrational but I didn't give half a fuck I needed to know.

"It was um, Robert, my ex fiancé." I could sense her discomfort and for the life of me I couldn't figure out why this shit should matter but it just did.
"How ex is ex?"
"Um, I broke up with him the day after we first met." That went right through me. That was sweet as fuck and said a lot but I'll have to come back to that later.

"Why?" I took a step closer to her taking her chin in my hand.

"Why?"
"Yes; why did you break up with him the day after you first met me?"
"You now why." Her face started to blush but I pushed on.
"Tell me." I held her eyes with mine reading the truth of her words there.
"Um because I knew I wasn't in love with him and that it wouldn't be fair."
"Good girl."

"Why did we have to come out here to talk?"
"Because I don't want talk of another man in my house, scratch that in our home. You don't have any dealings with him ever again."
"Connor."
"That's dead, not up for discussion he had you I don't want to ever hear his name pass your lips again; we clear?"

She swallowed hard and stared at me like I'd lost my mind. I very well might have but that's what's inside of me. The thought of that fucker whoever he is even breathing the same air as her fucked with my head. There's no way I'd ever believe that he wouldn't always want her.

The fact that she'd been the one to break things off told me that he probably wasn't completely out of the picture. I wouldn't believe that he wouldn't want her back. Knowing what I do now, how sweet she is, how she feels under me, around me, no fucking way. I wanted to know everything about their relationship. How long it had lasted, who'd approached who? But I didn't want to freak her out any more than I probably already had with my dominating ways, she'd find out soon enough.

"Were there any others?" The fuck Connor what's with you? She's a grown woman she wasn't sitting on a shelf somewhere waiting for your ass to come along. Doesn't matter I need to know.

"No." She turned bright red and looked at the ground.

I wasn't sure if that was worst or not. I took it in and decided to drop it for now. This shit would drive me nuts if I dwelt on it too much tonight. We were too new, still at that learning stage and I'm sure there were going to be many things from her past that I'd try to erase.

I'm territorial like that so the fuck what? I know my thinking was off, I wasn't a virgin last night either and I can't remember ever feeling this possessive of a woman before. But with her it was as if something inside me, something that had been hidden there had reared its head. The need to own her, to completely take her over in every way was strong. I look at her and all I think is 'mine' all fucking mine. "Let's go on inside it's getting chilly out here."

Chapter 6

With my arm thrown around her shoulders I led her back inside the house and to the den. Honestly all I really wanted was to drag her off to bed. But I didn't want her thinking that that was all she meant to me, women can be strange that way. So I forced myself to sit through a movie while sitting on the couch with my arms around her, my cock hard as fuck and wondering when he was gonna get to play with her again.

"Do you mind if I ask you something Connor?" She broke the silence halfway through the film that I'd been having trouble following because her scent was getting to me. "You can ask me anything love." I squeezed her shoulders.
"In that case I have lots of questions."

She turned that beautiful face up to me, eyes wide and bright and so beautiful she made my heart ache. I couldn't resist running my finger down her cheek and touching her lips softly with mine. "Shoot."

"Okay first, why do you all live here like this?"

"We're brothers, we made the decision a long time ago that when the time came we would do something like this. We didn't know where in the country we would've done it. We hadn't settled on any one place yet but we knew this is what we wanted. Then our commander died and left us this land so here we are." I didn't bother asking if she had a problem with the arrangement because nothing was going to change. I'll always live with my brothers and she'll always be with me. There was no point in debating it.

"Okay I think the town thinks you guys are some sort of gang or something. I mean they know you're ex military but what with the bikes and the fact that you guys are always together I think there's a little fear that you might be some kind of biker gang."

"Do you have that fear?"

"No, I like the fact that you guys are so close, it feels like you made your own family you know."

"That's exactly right baby we did and that's what makes it special, we had the choice and we chose each other. What's your next question?" She seemed to need some time to put this one into words so I squeezed her shoulder gently.

"Spit it out sweetheart it can't be that bad." She bit her lip and bowed her head a little.

"Why did you not want to be with me?" Her voice was barely above a whisper and I had to bend to hear her.

"Is that what you thought, that I didn't want you?" I had to look at her to gauge her sincerity; I can't believe she'd been that off. "Nothing could be farther from the truth sweetheart, I was trying to protect you."

"Protect me? Protect me from what?"

"Me." I lifted her face to mine so she could read the seriousness on my face. This was probably one of the most important conversations we'll ever have and I needed her to understand where I was coming from.

"I don't understand. Why would I need protection from you?"

"Because I'm not like most men baby. I live by my own set of rules I'm never going to be anyone's ideal of the perfect man. I don't believe in towing the line and falling in with everyone else. None of us do, our women are going to have to be strong to put up with our shit. I didn't think you were going to be able to deal with me."

"I still don't understand."

"I'm an all or nothing kind of guy babe. If you're with me you're with me all the way no half stepping no looking back. There might come a time when you fuck up and I can't promise things will be easy. I'm going to expect things from you that you might not be ready to give. I'll try to be patient but you're gonna have to learn real fast because last night we crossed the point of no return."

"What does that mean?"
"It means that I now own you, that you're mine one hundred percent. It means you do what I say when I say no questions." Her body tensed beneath my arm and I tried to soothe her.
"I'm not going to abuse you baby, it's not like that; it's just that I've seen enough shit in the world that I've learned to be careful. I don't want you to ever be in danger so if I tell you not to do something and you do it anyway it might set me off."

"And what happens then?"
Oh I could see I was scaring her now. It couldn't be helped though she needed to know the truth of what she was getting herself into.
"Then you get your little ass spanked for disobeying me and for putting

yourself in danger. I might overlook some things but that one's a no no."

She didn't seem to believe me so I nodded at her to let her know I was dead serious. She took a deep breath and just looked at me. She'd probably never been spanked a day in her life but I know me. I would have no problem taking a belt to her ass if she fucked up and put herself in danger. Hopefully we never got to that point ever because that's one thing I wasn't looking forward to.

"Don't worry about it baby just don't fuck up and you'll be fine."
"But how will I know?" She seemed really concerned about that so I set about trying to ease her fears.
"It's simple, no other men ever that's a given. You're free to do whatever you want to this isn't about that. But you will not go anywhere that I tell you not to. I'll need to know where you are at all times that one's not up for debate. It's more about your safety than my needing to control you though make no

mistake about it Danielle I will control you. It's the only way I can do this."

"You're scaring me."
"No need to be scared I'm here to protect you and take care of you. These are just some of the things you're gonna have to get used to being with me. I gave you plenty of chances to move on Danielle, you chose to stay. Don't think I missed all those signals babe, I didn't miss them and oh yeah. That little stunt you pulled the other day, don't do that shit again."

"What stunt was that?" Yeah like she didn't know. She yanked my chain to bring me to heal and she damn well knew it too. I can't fault her for going after what she wanted. "That day you walked right by me and pretended you didn't see me. You do some shit like that again it's gonna go very badly for you. I cant say as I liked the feeling too much so consider yourself warned. Now back to your safety. Try your best to never disobey me on that score and your ass should be safe from my belt but Danielle, the first time you break that rule will be the last you get me?"

She blushed and planted her face in my chest so I brushed her hair back soothingly. I had no doubt I was scaring the shit out of her but like I'd told her. I've seen some shit that would make the average man padlock himself in a house and never set foot among humanity ever again. There are some sick fuckers in the world and a lot of the time women find themselves at the wrong end of that evil shit. I don't know that she would ever be in that type of danger here in this little burgh but I wasn't willing to take the chance.

"Would you ever like, fold your fists and hit me?" I felt my heart clutch at her question as memories threatened to intrude, memories of the one who was supposed to protect becoming the monster. I've always believed that has to be a woman's worst nightmare. Something I could never find myself doing, I'd die first before I ever did that to her. It would kill me if I ever saw that fear and degradation in her eyes.

"No baby that's fucked, there're grown men who couldn't take one of my punches I could never come at you like that. But if you pissed me off and did something I didn't like I might tan your hide."
"Wow, I didn't know people actually did that."

" Fuck if I know what people do, but that's me. Like I said it's nothing for you to worry about just don't fuck up. There're only two things that might get me to that point. If you put yourself in danger or you fucked with another man. Outside of that your ass should be safe from my belt. As for me folding my fists and knocking you around, not only would I never do such a thing but my brothers would have my ass if I even thought of doing something like that."

"Okay, I feel better I don't think I'll be getting any beatings because I don't like putting myself in danger and I don't want anyone else but you." She turned her face up for my kiss and I took her lips willing myself to leave it at just one kiss and not jump her right then and there. The kiss heated up a little so I eased off and just held her close to me and we went back to watching the show.

It felt right sitting here with her like this too. I felt settled for the first time in my life, like everything had finally come together. As soon as the credits started rolling I turned the TV off though, my cock was about ready to rip out of my pants it was so hard.

"Time for bed." I was about to burst, it had been hours since I had her and I couldn't wait a second longer. "I'm going to have you now." I started stripping her on the way up the stairs my hands going straight to her ass. I knelt behind her for a better look.

"I love your ass it's so fucking perfect, sweet." I bit her on her cheek and she squealed and ran before turning back to me halfway up the stairs.

"I love everything about your body, it's so strong." She was off and running again, her face red. I caught up with her in the bedroom where we started hurriedly taking off the rest of our clothes. She ran her hands over my chest and arms with her head on my chest, as she seemed to be drawing in my scent. I pulled her in close and rubbed my naked cock against the softness of her stomach.

I was hard and hurting to get inside her. There wouldn't be any foreplay tonight. One finger inside her pussy told me she was wet enough to take my length without too much trouble. I'll take care of her after, but this first time I couldn't hold off.

"Hop up here." I pulled her up in my arms with her long legs wrapped around me her pussy right over my cock, her folds cradling me. Her hips started to move slowly up and down as she masturbated my cock against her clit and back down to her slit. Taking my cock in hand I lifted her enough to reach her opening and pulled her down on me filling her.

"Yeah right there baby, you're so fucking tight." I fucked her standing up lifting and dropping her on my cock as she moaned and clenched, her juices running down my thighs.
"Give me your mouth."

Making love to her felt like nothing I'd ever felt before, she fit me like a glove. Hot, wet and tight as I stood in the middle of the room with her impaled on my cock. I held onto her ass as I fucked up into her but pretty soon that wasn't enough. I needed to be deeper inside her. The mating hadn't been fulfilled yet it was going to take a while for me to feel like I'd staked my claim, almost like imprinting myself on her in her.

"Baby I want to do you from behind." Pulling her off my cock I turned her around and propped her over the bed. I ran my cock from her clit back to her ass before she reached back and opened herself with both hands inviting me into her pink sweetness. Fuck, my mouth watered at the sight and I wanted to suck on her pussy but not as much as I wanted to fuck her. I watched as my cock forced its way inside her going deep on the first plunge.

At her screech of ahh I held still until she grew accustomed to having me in her like this. I could feel how deep I was inside her as the tip of my cock butted against the rubbery flesh of her cervix before pulling back out. I had to close my eyes against the feelings that threatened to over power me. Fuck, being inside her felt like I'd found my place, like there was nowhere else I wanted to be. This was it for me she was it for me.

"Grab the sheets babe." She fisted the sheets and I started up again. Slow and steady getting her used to having me so deep inside her. Slow and steady, that's how we made love until the need became too much and I had to fuck.

With fistfuls of her ass cheeks in my hands I fucked my little southern belle the way I'd been wanting to ever since the moment I first laid eyes on her. I needed to stake my claim here and now to own her pussy, own her. Wrapping my hand around her throat I pulled her head back so I could tongue fuck her mouth. I wanted to do things to this girl that I've never done to anyone before but was she ready for it? There was only one way to find out.

"You're driving me crazy Danielle, what the fuck did you do to me?"

She didn't have a chance to answer because my hand was cutting off her circulation as I fucked into her wildly from behind. Her fingers dragged across the bed as her body shook with the force of my hips slamming into hers.

I kissed her again my tongue buried deep in her mouth as she sucked and fought for air her pussy clenching sweetly around me as her body struggled. I was totally out of control, couldn't get deep enough inside her hot little pussy. I wanted to brand her somehow; the need to completely control was overwhelming. This is why the debutante and the ex SEAL was a bad idea the shit I needed from her sexually would probably scare her half to death.

"I need to get deeper inside you fuck…I can't…I can't…fuck…" I went out of my head as her pussy tightened and she pushed back telling me without words that she was with me all the way. Thank fuck. I pulled

her hair hard pulling her head back
making a deeper arch in her back. The
only place we touched other than my
hand in her hair was my cock in her
pussy and my other hand cupping her
so I could force my fingers in there
with my cock.

My long pole going in and out of
her looked like I was sawing her in
two when I finally looked down at
where we were connected. She spread
her legs wider trying to ease the
pressure and I released her hair and
smacked her ass hard.

"Close them." She fucking came
from having her ass smacked fuck
yeah. My sweet innocent girl liked to
play rough. We'll see.
I pulled her hands behind her back
bent my knees and dipped deeper into
her.
"Have you ever been fucked in the ass
sweetheart?"
"No unghh." I couldn't believe how
well she was taking my pounding.
There was no whining about me being

too rough; in fact she seemed to revel in it as she moved her ass around and around on my cock changing up her movements. I know when I finally cum it's going to be a fucking tsunami.

"I need you to cum baby I'm there, cum for me."
I touched her clit and went deep one last time as she trembled and shook in orgasm. I caught her scream in my mouth pulling her head back roughly as I emptied my nuts deep inside her womb.

Chapter 7

After cleaning up and heading to bed I was finally able to relax for the first time that day. I hadn't realized that I'd been holding my breath waiting for something to go wrong to keep her from me. But she was here now and there was nothing that could take her away, I won't let it.

"Does your parents know you're here?"
"Um, yeah I told my mom."
"And what did she say?"
"She wasn't too happy about us living together without um, marriage but she respects the fact that I'm an adult."

"That's it? That's her only issue with us that we're not married?"
"Yeah."
"Well then she won't have to worry for too long because as soon as you can arrange it we'll tie the knot."

Her head flew up off my chest where she'd been busy at work drawing patterns with her fingers and making my dick twitch.
"You're going to marry me?" Why was she so fucking surprised?
"Uh yeah, what did you think we were doing here Danielle? I brought you home with me baby that should've told you something."

She ran her hand through her hair before gliding over my body to lie on my chest her face in mine.
"I don't know, I just never thought you would want to."
"So you were willing to live with me even if I wasn't offering marriage?"
"In case you haven't noticed Mr. Connor Malone I'm silly in love with you."

Now I'm the one damn near blushing. A woman like that tells you so effortlessly that she loves you can do things to a man. I suspected of

course but to hear her say it in her
sweet voice, no words.
"I know baby, I'm in love with you
too…don't cry come 'ere." I turned her
to my side and rolled so I could hold
her the way I wanted to. My leg
thrown over her hip my arms wrapped
securely around her sheltering her
from the world.

Damn how did I get so lucky?
First I met my brothers all those years
ago and we all just bonded for life.
Then the commander who'd been the
salt of the earth had pretty much taken
us under his wing all those years and
later leaving us this place. Now this,
the most beautiful woman in the world
was in love with me. It was almost too
good to be true. After the childhood
I'd had this was like a fairytale,
something you only saw in the movies.

When I was living in hell all
those years ago did I ever wish for
this? Did I ever dream it was possible?
I don't know but I do know I'm
holding on with both arms and I'll

fight to the death to keep my little piece of heaven. I pulled her in even closer inhaling her scent, running my hands over her body reveling in the fact that this was all mine.

"So it's settled we'll get married as soon as possible, there's just one thing. It's just my brothers and I none of us really have any family to speak of other than each other. My parents are long gone, well my mom is anyway I never met my dad he died before I was born. Logan's mom lives out West somewhere; she's a nice lady she kinda sees the rest of us as hers too since we're all pretty much orphans so I hope you won't be too embarrassed that my side of the church will be damn near empty."

"I don't care about that, I don't even care if we just go down to the courthouse and get it done I just want to be your wife."
"No, no courthouse. I'm sure you're one of those types who dreamt of her wedding day since she was knee high

to a grasshopper. Probably have your dream dress picked out and everything so no. You'll have your dream wedding, just give me a figure and I'll get you a check."

"No Connor..."
"Babe I know the people around here think we're poor soldiers but we're not hurting for cash. One of the things the commander did when we were younger was teach us how to manage our money very well. He taught us how to play the market among other things to safeguard our funds. Now Quinn is better at that shit than the rest of us so he handles that, but trust me none of us are hurting and the business as young as it is is doing pretty good. We have enough contracts to see us through a good couple years so I don't want you to worry okay."

"Okay, but you do know the bride's family is supposed to pay for the wedding right? It's tradition."
Fuck I know about weddings and shit?
"If it's tradition and they want to then

by all means I won't stand in their way, but I want to contribute as well. Now lets get some sleep we both have work tomorrow.

"Connor?"
"Yeah sweetie?" I squeezed her shoulders.
"Would you like to meet my mom and dad?"
"I'd love to meet your parents." Shit I've never met anyone's parents before. I'd joined the service straight out of high school and the girls I'd messed around with back then weren't the sort that you had to meet their parents. The poor boy from the wrong part of town didn't exactly mix with the higher ups. Now look where I'd landed; with the cream of the fucking crop.

She likes to take care of me. That's the first thing I noticed the next morning when I went downstairs after my shower. I'd had her up against the wall in the shower stall as the water poured down on us. Her legs wrapped around my waist as I went in and out of her stroking nice and easy. I could get used to this shit, having her pussy first thing in the morning. The only reason I hadn't had her again during the night is because I knew she had to be sore. Hard fucking two nights in a row would do that to you.

So I'd behaved like the perfect gentleman all through the night only allowing myself to cup her pussy as I slept behind her. A few finger thrusts while I rubbed my leaky cock against her fine ass was all I allowed myself but as soon as morning came I was in that pussy again. I hope she didn't get tired of me fucking her anytime soon because I seriously didn't see any let up in sight anytime in the near future.

And as sweet as her pussy was shit, morning evening noon and night is what I'm thinking.

In the kitchen she was making me breakfast, already dressed in her silk blouse and linen skirt and high heels that made her calves look amazing. She wore pearls around her neck and that damn perfume that made me hard as a fucking rock. She was busy making me bacon and eggs with toast and potatoes and all I could do was shake my head. She couldn't be real, the whole fucking package and she'd just dropped right into my fucking lap.

"Hey honey I'm making you breakfast, a nice southern spread. You didn't have any grits in the cupboard so I'll pick some up later." She turned to me over her shoulder with that smile of hers.

"Not sure about the grits sweetheart."

"You'll love my cheesy grits honey I promise." That sugar sweet voice of hers. I was looking forward to listening to that for the rest of my life. She had to scratch her leg or something and as she lifted the edge of her skirt I caught sight of the top of thigh highs with a garter belt.

"That's it turn off the stove."

"Huh?" She didn't have time for anything else because my mouth came down on hers and I consumed her with a kiss before turning her around in front of the sink. I lifted her skirt pushed the seat of her panties aside and wrestled with my zipper freeing my cock and slamming into her.

She squealed and her body shook.

"Fuck baby did I hurt you?"

"No keep going I like it, I like the way you lose control." She was already out of breath and her pussy was doing its thing sucking my cock in.

"You drive me fucking crazy, your pussy is so good baby. I'll try to be quick and not mess up your clothes." I wasn't sure about her skirt though because my hands were rough as I pushed it up higher around her waist. The sight of those damn garters made me ravenous.

"From now on you have to always wear garters under your skirts and dresses." I pounded into her pushing her body into the edge of the sink with each thrust. I wanted to go slow but fuck I couldn't it was as if my dick had a mind of its own. He was on some seek and conquer mission or some shit. Or it could just be that her pussy owned us.

"Fuck baby why can't I ever get deep enough inside you?" It was true, no matter how far inside her I went I wanted to get deeper. The picture we made was highly erotic. Like an old fashioned story the lady of the manor and the stable boy. We were so completely opposite to each other in every way.

The sight of my large work roughened hands on her peaches and cream skin made me even harder inside her. This is why I was sure it was going to take some time before I got enough of her. Why I was pretty sure I was going to be in her as often as I could get my cock up. That contrast, the way she fulfilled every dream I never even knew I had. I bit into her neck too overcome to do anything else before I growled like a wild beast and emptied inside her. When I finally pulled out after her body settled, she was a limp mess.

"Oh shoot I'm leaking." She cupped her pussy as she ran to the downstairs bath to clean up. She was such a funny sight toddling on her heels skirt tucked up around her waist as she tried to catch my sperm as it ran out of her…oh fuck. I sat down hard in the chair. I hadn't worn a condom. Again. It seems like I was always forgetting. Or was I subconsciously trying to tie her down? I've never ridden bareback with anyone else before, not once in thirty-four years. How could I not have remembered? But she felt so fucking good. I knew it was gonna happen. Knew I was gonna work towards that eventually but we hadn't talked about it. Fuck. I was at least going to give her a few months to get settled in here before planting my kid in her.

"What's wrong Connor why aren't you eating?" She went to get me coffee when she reentered the room. "Sweetie are you on birth control?" She stopped short and looked at me like Bambi caught in the headlights. "No, I'm allergic so the few times I uh, ahem…we used a condom."

"What do you mean the few times wasn't it a regular thing?" "Um no, you see…you sure you want to bring that up in here?"

"You're right let's head out back." She brought her coffee and I took mine. You'll never guess that she was just bent over the kitchen sink getting drilled hard. She was all put together not a hair out of place.

"Okay so tell me."
"Robert and I dated in high school that's when we uh, you know. Then I went away to school and so did he and we kind of grew apart until a year ago when we met again and hit it off."

" Don't say his name…go on you went away to school, and…" I wasn't too jazzed about hearing about this shit first thing in the morning and especially not after having just fucked my woman but I guess she had a point to make.

"Well, I wasn't in a rush to hop back into bed with him, maybe that should've told me something." She mumbled that last part to herself but I heard her loud and clear.

"Anyway I decided I wanted to wait until after the wedding. It's one thing to experiment when you're a teenager with hormones making you crazy and quite another as a grown woman who wants to do things right."

"Uh babe I fucked you on our first date, in fact that wasn't even a date."
"Yeah but I didn't have a choice you just took me over."
"Any regrets?"
"Nope I wouldn't change a thing."

"So he had you when you were eighteen, fine I can live with that that brings us back to the birth control thing."
"I'm sorry I forgot."
"Not your fault sweetheart we'll deal with it as it comes."
"Would you be terribly upset if I was?"

I had to think about that seriously for a minute, fatherhood. It wasn't something I'd ever given much thought to that's for sure. Until her, I could see us raising a couple kids together very happily. Before I could answer though I saw six strapping men heading our way.

"Shit brace yourself here comes my nosy ass brothers."
She shifted her body closer to mine as the men drew near and I felt it in the gut. She'd done that shit subconsciously, just gravitated to me. I liked the fuck out of that shit. My arm went around her shoulders as they stopped in front of us.

"Unhand the beauty brother it's our turn. Hello Danielle we're the brothers, I'm Logan, this is Zak, Tyler, Quinn, Cord and Devon." Each guy came forward to give her a hug. I was watching to make sure she didn't become too overwhelmed by the hulks but she seemed to be holding her own. She'd met them before of course the night of the party but this was different, now she was being greeted as the new little sister.

"Welcome to the family lil sister."

"Why thank you Zak that's mighty nice of you."

"Do you cook?"

"Geez Tyler, she just got here don't run her off with your appetite already." Cord punched him in the arm. Ty is a greedy fuck. Next to combat, eating is his favorite thing; it's a running joke among us. Tyler just shrugged off Cord's ribbing as per usual that boy made no bones about his eating habits.

"As a matter of fact I do. Why don't you boys come on over to our house for dinner tonight around seven? That'll give me plenty of time to put together something nice."

Our house, like the sound of that too.

Their mouths were all hanging open in shock and I have to say I was a little dumbstruck myself. Not that I'd expected her to snub them or anything. It's just I have these ideas in my head

of a southern debutante which she was
to the bottom of her tiny little feet. But
she's been smashing them left and
right. Full of surprises my little
Danielle.

"What is it, what are y'all staring
at?"
"You're gonna cook for us, all of us?"
"Why yes Quinn I am. Now are there
any allergies or any dislikes I should
know about?"
"Turnips I hate fu…uh freaking
turnips."

"That's alright Devon you can
swear I hate turnips myself nasty
things."
I was pretty proud of my girl as my
brothers beamed at her and her
generosity. "Alright clear out I have to
get my girl to work I'll see you lot in a
little bit." I led her back inside while
the others went about their business.
Breakfast was cold by now but I still
wolfed mine down while she picked at
hers. "You ready to head out babe?" I
took the dishes to the sink and rinsed

before putting them in the machine. "Come on you'll be late."

"Connor you don't have to take me it's no trouble for the car to come pick me up here." She stood to get her brief case and purse before following me out the door.
"No way baby I'm going to be away from you all day let me enjoy these last few minutes."

I got a kiss for that before helping her into the truck; I stole another one when I belted her into her seat. Can't stay away from her, it's going to be hell being away from her all day. Maybe the guys were right and I needed to take some time off and just spend it inside her until this gnawing need was at least under control.

"So what is it that you do anyway?"
"My family runs a charity and I'm the new vice president under mom."
"Yeah? What kind of things do you do I'm not too familiar with this stuff?" I

held her hand in mine as I maneuvered in and out of traffic.

"We raise funds for different causes like the new wing at the hospital that's so badly needed, that's our latest project. Um sometimes I have to attend state dinners and throw parties but we usually use the estate for that."
"You like it?"
"I love it, it's very fulfilling being able to help others who're in need."

We talked about our jobs and shared some childhood stories, which I steered more towards hers than mine. My childhood was fucked and not something I was in too much of a hurry to share.

Hers sounded like something out of a fairy tale, which is what I kind of expected. She'd grown up with the American dream. Cheerleader, junior pageants, which she seemed a bit embarrassed about and family vacations. That was great at least one of us will have something like that to pass on to our kids.

"It sounds perfect babe. Makes me wonder why you'd ever want to get tangled up with the likes of me; don't answer that it's too late now. I've had a taste of you now and you're stuck." She blushed and hid her head in my shoulder, which meant I had to kiss her hair.

I dropped her off at the front of her office building and watched her walk in before turning around and heading to the site. Fucking unreal. I'm in jeans and work boots and my woman wears silk and pearls. I had a big stupid ass grin on my face as I pulled onto the lot though.

Logan the unofficial head of our little family came to meet me as I climbed out of the truck.
"You did good brother she's a keeper."
"Yeah it's unbelievable. Who knows maybe there's hope for you and your girl."

"Nah I don't think it's in the cards for me brother but I'm happy for you though."

Hardheaded fuck. I decided to leave it alone for now but I knew that if I could find my perfect girl there was nothing stopping my brothers from doing the same. A week ago I would've been singing a different tune but now shit, my Danielle is starting to make me believe in miracles.

Chapter 8

I got caught up in measurements and fittings as the morning progressed. The first floor of the structure was almost complete we had six more floors to go. Pretty soon we were going to have to hire more hands because the work was pouring in but we needed to find the best. We'd already discussed it, with the recession in full swing there were plenty of people looking for work but we had to take our time and sift through until we found the perfect fit. We'd all decided our first choice were vets we knew better than most how much they needed it. But that's another story for another time.

"Who's making the lunch run?" Shit time had flown, I'd been so caught up in my head I hadn't realized it was that time already. Just a few more hours and she'll be back in my arms. Geez Malone when did you become a bitch? I shook my head at my inner musings I've been doing that a lot lately, talking to myself.

"I think it's lover boy's turn." I threw a piece of wood at Tyler, which he ducked.
"Fine I'll go what do you animals want?" I pulled off my work gloves and took a swig from my water bottle.
"Turkey club for me extra mayo."
"Yes Logan we know you have the same damn thing everyday."

I took their orders and headed off to the center of town where the only decent restaurant was located. I called in the order on the way so it would be ready for pickup when I got there. This way I could just park out front and run in; a quick in and out.

I walked right up to the counter where the middle-aged waitress Anita was getting my stuff together and got an idea. Pulling my phone I called her.

"Hey sweetie did you have lunch?"

"Not yet I'm swamped, I think maybe I'll grab something a little later."
"How do I get to you?"
"Just ask at the front desk."

She sounded excited which made me feel like I'd made the right call. I ordered her the salad she asked for and added a sandwich. I don't think salad was a substantial enough meal for lunch. I exchanged small talk with Anita while I waited for them to fill the new order before heading out.

At the front desk they were expecting me and I headed up to her office. She was all smiles when she saw me and got up from her desk to greet me.
"Hi."
"Hi." I couldn't help kissing her so I did just that. I pulled her in close and kissed her, her taste going straight to my dick.

"Well now Danielle I sure hope that's your Connor."

She pulled away red in the face. "Momma shh."

There was an older woman maybe in her forties standing in the doorway smiling at us. She was tiny like her daughter but that's where the similarities ended. Where my Dani was dark she was light. I guess she must look like her dad, which would make him one beautiful man.

"I can see the questions Mr. Connor. She takes after her great great grandmother on her father's side she got none of me or her daddy." "Momma this is Connor, Connor this is my mom Catherine." "Pleased to meet you ma'am."

"The pleasure's all mine son now my girl has been buzzing all day about a wedding. I know you're just here to bring her lunch but maybe one evening soon you two can come up to the house and we can go over some things. Her daddy might need some working on. He's very fond of his little girl he isn't going to take too kindly to her living in sin, so I'm thinking we'd better get this wedding business squared away right quick."

"Yes ma'am how about Friday night? We already have plans for this evening."
"That'll be just fine gives me time to soften him up a bit, Jeremiah's bark is worse than his bite not to worry." She patted my shoulder before leaving us again.

"So I guess I'll see you later, you need to pick up anything for tonight?"
"Yes I do so maybe I can leave a little earlier. It's no problem for me to get a ride to the store and back to your place except…"
"Except what?" I pushed the hair back from her face as she bit her lip looking embarrassed again.
"I don't have a key."
"Shit how could I be so stupid?" I took my house key off the chain and passed it off to her with some cash.

"I'll see you around five then I guess, you call me if you need anything."
"I will thanks honey."
Damn. I stole one more kiss before leaving her.

"What took you so long bro?"
"Shut up Ty, come and get it boys." I passed out their food and ignored the looks.
"You went to see her didn't you?"
"Not that it's any of your business Zak but yes, I took my girl some lunch. Anything else you nosy asses want to know?"
"Yes does she have a sister, any friends?"
"No find your own woman brother; I met the mother, we're having dinner with her folks Friday night."
"How was the mother?" That was Logan for you get right to the heart of the matter.

"She was actually pretty cool, nothing at all like I expected." I gave Logan a pointed look, which he ignored.

They went about their lunch asking me a million and one questions like they'd never had a woman before. Granted she was the first of the sisters, we all knew that whatever women we brought into our midst had to fit in. And since she'd won them over this morning and was cooking for them tonight she was already off to a good start. They seemed almost as excited as I was to have her with us. Poor thing I hope she could keep up with this bunch.

That evening when I got to the house the smells hit me at the door. She was in the kitchen wearing soft worn jeans and a t-shirt. This time she had diamond studs in her ears and her hair was up in a sexy ponytail high on her head. She looked like a high school cheerleader. All soft and pink and fresh like she'd just left the shower. I walked over and wrapped her in my arms from behind, dirty work clothes and all.

"Hey you."
That smile she turned up to me always hits me in the heart. I wonder how long it'll take me to get used to the idea of her, of us. It still seems so unreal, like I'm going to wake up any moment to find it was all just a dream.

"I love you Danielle Susannah." There I'd said it first and nothing blew the fuck up. Somehow saying it first felt different to just saying I love you too. That's probably why my gut felt like it was tied in knots bigger than my fist. I never thought I'd be saying that shit to anyone. But I'm a man who believes in facing shit head on. I'm in love with her all the way, totally and completely gone.

"I love you more." She nibbled on my lip as she turned in my arms. "I doubt it but it's good you think so. I'm gonna go clean up and come help you, I expect those animals will be here soon."
"That's no problem I've got it under control. I got some beer and stuff for you guys, I wasn't sure what you liked so I got a mix."
"Damn are you sure you're real? What are you making anyway?"

"Chicken fried chicken with peppered gravy, skillet cornbread, fried okra and baked macaroni."
"Geez baby that shit sounds like a lot of work. You sure you don't need me to do anything?"
" Nope I've got it all taken care of I like doing this stuff don't worry. You

go get yourself together and come keep me company."

"You're the best." I stole one more kiss before heading upstairs for my shower.

The guys were showing up when I came back downstairs. Ty of course was one of the first. I could sense the melancholy in him. He was probably thinking about his own Georgia peach. The little filly has been giving him the eye since we got here but like me he was playing it safe.

Feeling the way I feel today I have no idea why I fought it so hard. Hopefully he wouldn't wait too long to come to his senses. I didn't even try to bring that shit up though because he'll just shoot me down. My brothers are very good at sticking their noses in but when it comes to getting them to take their own advice it's like pulling teeth.

Pretty soon the kitchen was full of people as us guys stood around with beers in hand shooting the breeze. The atmosphere was light, the air sweet with her scent and the food she was making. She'd set the dining room table with these fancy dishes that I guess she brought over with her.

"You didn't need to break out the good china for this bunch babe, they would've been fine with paper plates." "They're our first guests Connor be civil." She bumped me out of the way with her hip.

"He's two minutes out the cave little sister don't pay him no mind." Cord grinned at the left hook I halfheartedly threw his way.

We headed out back while she finished doing her thing. The talk had turned to the trouble that was brewing in the town and since she wasn't going to be touched by that shit ever we headed out of hearing distance. That's sort of an unspoken rule among the men.

Our women, no matter who they maybe are to be sheltered from the fuckery of the world. It's a bit archaic but who gives a fuck? It's who we are and any woman we ended up with will have to understand. Danielle with her soft sweet as pie ass did not need to be dealing with drug trafficking and criminal bullshit. As my woman her biggest worry in life from now on should be what the fuck to wear, that's it and I don't give a fuck who agrees.

They still hadn't been able to find anything that would help us get to the bottom of what was going on. There was evidence of activity down on the pier but the few nights the guys had staked out the place without me they hadn't found anything suspicious.

"So what's our next move?" "Fuck if I know but we have to do something soon before those old guys decide to take things into their own hands, that won't be good." Logan swigged his beer as the rest of us sat around my back patio overlooking the pool. It gave me ideas about late night skinny-dipping with my girl. I'll have to gag her though if we were going to be doing anything more than swimming because she can get loud when shit gets hot. And Danielle naked in a pool beneath the stars, shit will definitely get hot fast.

I tuned back into the conversation when my body started responding to the shit in my head. "Well we definitely know something's going on there but what? Is it drugs, human trafficking, what? There isn't anyone here that sends up a red flag and we've looked into the towns around us. There's some potential there but nothing we can pin down. I say we set up some sort of surveillance out there and see what we get."

"I like that idea Ty, I don't want anything fucking up our little paradise here." Devon was the youngest by a year. Of all of us he must've had the best childhood until he was fourteen and his parents got killed in a car crash. Then shit went to hell fast when he ended up with a drunken uncle who liked talking with his fists. He was the only who had grown up with a family and if not stellar surroundings at least they were better than the rest of us had. I thought for sure he would be the first to settle down because it's all he's ever wanted. To get out and find a nice woman and set up shop in a nice place, a place like this.

"Maybe we should've called the cops let them handle it, we're civilians now remember?"
"We'll never be just civilians Cord and besides we don't have anything to take

to the cops except rumors that we ourselves have yet to substantiate. No I think Ty has the right idea, we just have to find the best way to do that shit. I hear your woman coming bro." Logan turned to the door just as she appeared. Ears like a fucking hawk. "Food's ready boys."

There was a stampede into the house where she had a spread set out family style in the never before used dining room. I think we all stood around for a good minute after she was seated, just taking it in before grabbing our own seats. She'd gone out of her way to make it nice. The table was set and there were flower petals of all things strewn across the top of it. She'd even put little tea candles in glass jars with marbles or some shit in the bottoms in the middle of it. I felt like a proud husband every time my brothers complimented her on her efforts.

"Man Danielle, are you hung up on this guy? Because I'm just as good looking as he is."

"Shut up Ty, hands off my girl."

"Can't blame a guy for trying."

"Thanks for the compliment Ty that's very sweet."

"So what's for dessert?"

"You're a pig bro."

"What? I know this nice southern girl wouldn't serve us dinner without dessert."

"And you will be right, I made a nice pecan pie, we'll have it with some vanilla bean ice cream."

"Sweet."

"You guys have KP." I warned the greedy fucks as they cleaned their plates.

"For a meal like this I'll even mop the floor." Devon was forking food into his mouth like it was his last meal.

Chapter 9

Later that night after all was quiet again I had her on her hands and knees on the bathroom floor. It was wild and deep and out of control. She'd taken a shower and was putting moisturizer on her face when I came in and got a look at her, with just a towel wrapped around her.

I'd only meant to nibble on her neck and cop a feel. But the towel slipped and I got a feel of her flesh and that's all it took for me to take her down. I ate her pussy while she leaned over the vanity counter, until she leaked into my mouth. Her hand reached back pulling my face into her as I tongued her clit before burying my tongue deep inside her.

When she begged me in her sweet voice to fuck her I'd almost lost it and that's how she ended up in this predicament. I had no doubt her knees were hurting on the hard marble floor as I pounded into her without let up.

"Hold on baby this is gonna be short and sweet." Her ass bounced with each plunge of my cock, and when she leaned her shoulders closer to the floor I went deeper. I could see the pink of her pussy as my cock pulled out.

"I want to fuck your ass so bad baby, fuck." Just the thought of my cock slicing through her sweet ass brought me to the brink. I guess she liked the idea as well because she screamed. Her pussy locked me inside and I felt the hot rush of her pussy's sweetness as she came and came while I kept plowing away unit my cock was dry heaving into her.

We were both breathless and limp but I had enough strength left to pick her up and take her to bed.

"I don't want you to wash my scent off of you. I want to hold you all night with my cum inside you."
She cooed and buried her face in my neck.

Life was damn near perfect for the next few days as we got into the groove of living together. We moved around each other like we'd been doing it for a long time. We fucked more than we did anything else in that first week. Our dinner at her parents' place had been postponed because her dad had to go out of town for a business matter and her mom apparently always traveled with him. It was a family tradition she said she wanted us to keep as well. Never spending the night away from each other. I could get with that no problem.

She had all these cute little quirks that I just fell in love with the more time we spent together. Like the way she twitched her nose when she watched TV. Or the way she held her tongue between her teeth when she was concentrating really hard on something. I found myself touching her all the time for no reason other than that I could. I especially love the way she curls herself around me in bed when it's time to sleep. It's getting so I can hardly remember not having her there with me. She'd worked herself completely into my life in just a short space of time.

My brothers too treated her like she'd always been a part of our family. They spent the evenings regaling her with tales of my wayward past until I kicked them all out. She'd cooked for them three evenings out of the last six she was here and I was ready to tell them to quit, until she let me know she really enjoyed it. Seems my girl likes trying out her culinary skills on her new brothers. And they were only too happy to let her.

So that's where we were a week after the big move. She was settling in, I was learning how to live with someone female. Which was easier than I'd thought it would be. I loved seeing her makeup bottles and perfume and what not scattered around the bathroom counter. Or seeing her clothes hanging next to mine.

I guess it was a good thing I'd learned to be tidy in the Navy because my baby was not into tidying up. She was use to having maids and shit to do that for her so it was taking her a while to get into the habit of picking up behind herself. She had no shame in admitting that though she loved to cook she hated everything else that had to do with housekeeping. Laundry was her worst nightmare. She was so cute as she tried to figure out the washing machine while I stood in the door of the laundry room watching her.

When she gets flustered and frustrated she cusses, but not your average cuss words. No my woman's too well bred for that. She says things like bugger and drat and frak. Cute as hell.

"Baby I'm going to be gone for a little bit tonight okay. You'll be fine here by yourself. Unless you want to call Candy over for company."
"I just might do that I haven't seen her since I moved in. She comes to the office after I've gone and leaves before I get home in the evenings."
"Good then you should call her up."
"Will do."

She didn't bother asking me where I was headed because I'd told her that sometimes the guys and I had to go out in the evenings. I'd only told her a little of what we were doing, there was no sense in scaring her. And besides like I said I'm of the mindset that there're just some things a woman doesn't need to worry about.

My brothers and I have been patrolling the boardwalk for the past

142 | JORDAN SILVER

few nights but still we hadn't seen anything that we could use. There was definitely more foot traffic there after sunset but nothing to give us reason to believe there was anything illegal going down. Still the old man who had come to us didn't strike me as a flake so we didn't want to give up too soon. Could be someone had gotten wind of our presence and was watching and waiting. If that was the case then we were going to have to change shit up.

We took our bikes down to the pier. The boardwalk had been fixed up sometime in the last two years and there was talk of putting up rides and shit for the kids. But for now there were just a few benches here and there along the rail that overlooked the water and a few flowerpots. Someone was making noise about building a little ice cream shop down here, which wouldn't hurt. There was room for a lot of development but I'm not sure what if anything was going to happen. Right now our only interest is in keeping the riffraff out.

Briarwood was a quiet little town. The history wasn't as rich as some of its neighbors but it had seen its colorful days. The coast had once been a haven for pirates who made it this far down from the keys and as legend has it, there had been plenty of smuggling going on back then too.

Like most southern towns it had the taint of slavery attached to its history but today it was a diverse place with the descendants of both parties still in existence if old man Connelly was to be believed. He was something of the town historian. He and his crew of four hung around at the lodge or the local restaurant telling tall tales. These days they were more concerned with the goings on down here by the water.

"I see tracks over here but that could be anybody, maybe high school kids fooling around out here."
We'd spread out over the grassy area above the water's edge. The pier went out about fifty feet, not long by any means but this little inlet didn't need much more than that.

Leading off to the sides were grassy areas that could do with cutting. At the end was a little wooden building that had been closed since the repairs. There was space underneath where you could walk on the sand if the water wasn't too high and that's where we concentrated our efforts next.

If anyone was meeting out here for illegal purposes this would be the best place for them to hide. It was out of sight of anyone coming in either direction and with the absence of any lights it was more than suitable for a meet. Old man Connelly had said he was sure this is where they were meeting whoever they were. But so far we had yet to see any evidence of that in the few weeks we'd been on the lookout. There was never anything left behind to say that someone had been here.

"We've got cigarette butts." Devon was crouched down with a penlight pointed towards the ground. We'd left our bikes and walked in on the off chance that tonight would be our lucky night and we'd actually catch the culprits in the act. It wouldn't do to show our hand too soon. Seven men showing up on bikes might tip them off.

We all gathered around the place where Dev indicated.

"That could be anyone bro, high school kids smoke too you know."

"Yes Quinn I know but I don't think they're hiding under piers in the dark to do it. These weren't here the last time we were out here. I say we bag them and see what we see."

"Do it." Logan passed him a napkin to wrap the three butts in and we searched the area for anything else that might've been left behind that we could possibly use. It was a far cry from our assignments in the service. At least there was no threat of imminent danger. Not yet anyway, piece of cake.

"We get a brand off those butts Dev?" Devon studied one of the butts he'd picked up with tweezers and studied it under the penlight.

"Shit this is no kid bro. These are Dunhill Blue. Imports and a little too expensive for your average high school punk." Well shit. I was hoping against hope that there was nothing here. Even with everything I've seen in life I was really hoping not to have to deal with fuckery for at least the next little while, and especially not in my own backyard. But there could be no valid reason for anyone to be in this particular spot unless they were up to no good.

"So they were here since the last time we were; fuck. Looks like we've got something here after all guys maybe we should look a little more see what else we come up with." We spent a good hour scouring the brush with no luck before Logan called a halt. I was ready to get back to my woman anyway.

"I still say we figure out how to set up surveillance out here the sooner the better. I have a bad feeling about this even though we haven't seen anything so far. In fact that in itself bothers the fuck outta me. If whoever this is is good enough to hide from us then this is no small town outfit. This could be serious shit." Tyler looked around at the quiet around us where darkness had fallen hard in the last hour or so that we'd been out here.

"I'm with you brother something's going on. I just can't quite put my finger on it yet. But right now I just want to get home to my woman doesn't look like anything is going down here tonight."
"That's right brother rub it in."

There was a lot of ribbing and bullshitting around as we headed back to our bikes and headed for home. I knew the guys were just teasing but I couldn't help feeling a little sad that they hadn't found what I had. Not for lack of the local female population trying. My brothers have never had a problem attracting the ladies, none of us have. But like me they were all set in their ways and the women who caught them were going to have to be something special; like my Danielle. Damn it felt good knowing I was heading home to her.

"Baby where are you?" I called out for her as soon as I entered the house. After years of living alone it sure felt good to have someone to come home to. The fact that she was the sexiest thing on two legs was just the icing on the cake. I dropped my jacket over a chair in the kitchen as I walked through the house. There were no lights on downstairs except for a little side lamp that she'd no doubt left on for me.

Damn I don't remember anyone doing something so simply thoughtful for me except for my brothers, in a long time if ever. My mother sure never had. But I wasn't about to let thoughts of her and any of the bullshit from my past intrude here. All I wanted was my girl.

She was in the bedroom on the bed surrounded by a ton of papers. "What's up baby what're you doing?"

"It's for work I have to send a proposal and they want all this information before they will even consider supporting the project."
I leaned over her to take her mouth, felt like I hadn't kissed her in way too long.

"Find anything?"
"Not gonna answer that babe, I told you before I left the only reason I told you where I was going is because you need to know your man is not out there doing you wrong, but you don't get involved in this no way no how."
"But maybe I can help I do know the area better than you guys."

I looked at her long enough that she could get the seriousness of what I was about to say to her.
"You don't ever get involved in this do you understand me? It's not exactly Baghdad; if my brothers and I can handle that shit then we can certainly handle whatever is going on here. Now that's the last time we're gonna discuss it and Danielle, don't question me

again. I told you before if I tell you not to do something it's for your own good."

She didn't look too pleased but she backed down, good girl. I don't want her anywhere near anything that could be potentially dangerous, that's what she has me for to stand between her and danger. There was no give in me on that.

Having seen the shit I've seen over the years I know how important it is to protect what's mine. Someone like her who I'm sure have been sheltered her whole life wouldn't understand but in time hopefully she will. "I'm hopping in the shower be right back." One long hot kiss and I was gone.

I took my shower while she finished up her paperwork before bed. I didn't even bother with pajamas just came into the bedroom with my dick swinging. She was lying there waiting for me. I took a moment to study her as she reclined against the pillows.

Her hair spread out in a wild untamed mess and her long legs looking sexy as sin beneath the tail of my oversized shirt. She must've felt my stare because she turned to me, a smile breaking out across her magnificently beautiful face. My heart gave a little tug as I grinned back at her. I can't believe she's mine. If I'd ever wished for anything I could've never imagined her.

"Lose the shirt baby." I walked towards the bed purposefully, her eyes following my every move. I saw the flush of heat as she pulled the shirt off over her head, exposing her beautiful breasts and her newly waxed pussy. I'm going to be a real pig tonight because the sight of her made me iron hard and my mouth water. "Open your legs for me."

She spread herself open for me to climb between her thighs. I started at her smooth pussy lips licking her with my tongue. She tasted sweet and spicy as I slipped it farther inside. Lifting her ass in my hands I ate her as she lost all control and fucked my tongue hard. My cock was more than ready for some action so I made my way up her body. I teased her navel with my cock tip before grabbing my swollen cock and straddling her chest so she could suck me off.

Her mouth opened and she swallowed my cock head licking the pre cum. She took me in and sucked me deeper into her throat. I wanted so badly to fuck her face but she wasn't ready for that shit yet so I eased off. There was cock juice and spit running down her chin onto her chest as I fucked back and forth into her mouth slowly. My hands held her head in place for my thrusts; her cheeks were puffed out her throat working overtime.

"That's good baby." I eased out of her mouth and kissed my way down her chest nibbling on her nipples and fingering her pussy until I was in position between her thighs. I felt around for her pussy opening with my cock head before pushing in.

"You okay baby?" She made this hurt noise when I pushed into her like maybe I'd gone too deep too fast so I held still.
"Give me your mouth." She lifted her head so I could take her lips as I started moving.
"Open your legs wider."

She pulled her legs open and held them up with her arms as I dug deeper into her. "Your fucking pussy babe, what the fuck?" I didn't know a pussy could feel this good, like I never wanted to leave the sweet haven of her body. The cute little noises she made only made me want to pound her harder, faster. I slammed into her with each thrust her pussy's grip tight. Her eyes held mine, and her mouth was opened in amazement as she fucked back at me.

"Hold up your tit for me babe." She lifted her breast up for my mouth to explore. I sucked on her plump nipple and my cock grew even longer and harder inside her. I ground into her trying to bury my cock in the end of her. Her nails down my back, and her heels digging into my ass trying to get me even deeper inside her was just adding fuel to the fire.

"I'm cumming Connor, ahhh." She tightened around me just before I felt her release around me.
"Again, I want you to cum again." One hand went to her clit to help her along. Her body was flush with heat as she sought release.

"I'm glad you're not on birth control, I want to plant a kid in you. I'm going to plant a kid in you." The thought of breeding her made me fuck her harder. Lifting her ass in my hands I pulled her tighter to me as I buried my face in her neck and sucked.

She scratched my back hard as I pulled the flesh of her neck between my teeth.

"Yeah baby that's right cum for me." She came with a loud cry and I emptied inside her. Once again I didn't let her go clean up but pulled her into my side to sleep.

Chapter 10

We went through what was fast becoming our morning routine the next day. Except this morning there was a knock on the door and Ty came in. My girl didn't miss a beat just stepped over to the fridge and got more eggs. I was about to give him the stink eye to get him out. He was messing with my morning kitchen sex. But he was soon joined by the others so there was no point. These fuckers have no shame. They each pulled up a chair after grabbing a cup of coffee as if they were invited.

"Morning folks, sorry but this bunch smelt cinnamon rolls and there was no stopping them, I tried bro." "Yeah thanks Logan I'm sure you tried really hard." Cock blocking fucks. "Dude homemade cinnamon rolls that's almost worth breaking the bro code. They smell amazing Danielle." "Thanks Logan there's more than enough I made plenty." She seemed happy enough to have them all here waiting to be fed as she opened the oven and removed the savory offerings. I thought Ty would snatch the plate from her hand with his greedy impatient ass.

They fell on them like starving wolves and pretty soon the plate of twenty or more was clean. She made a mountain of eggs and rashes of bacon while I made another pot of coffee.

"You freaks better not make this a habit."

"No deal bro, this shit is too good. Don't mean to sound sexist Danielle but as the only lil sister around here looks like you're going to be having cook duty." Ty was busy stuffing his face as usual the pig.
"The hell she is, go get your own woman to cook for you."
"Selfish bro, that's just plain selfish and mean."
"Whatever."

We cleaned up the kitchen when we were done and I headed out behind them to take her to work. We held hands the whole drive over as we talked about what she wanted to do that evening. I had yet to take my woman on a date but she seemed content to just stay in for now. Fine by me, I'm not the out and about type but I'm sure she was accustomed to that shit.

"I'll see you later baby." She leaned over for her kiss and I tried not to suck her face off.
"Later."
I watched her walk in and then headed to work feeling lighter than I ever have in my life.

There was no time for mooning over my girl the rest of the morning I had shit to do. I volunteered to make the lunch run even though it wasn't my turn, which opened a shit storm of bullshit.

"Okay lover boy just don't forget to bring back lunch."
"Fuck off Zak."

"Say hello to our girl bro."
"What makes you guys so sure that
I'm going to see her?"
"Uh, you volunteered to make a lunch
run dude, dead give away."
"Whatever I'll be back."

I called ahead as usual and
placed my order with a little something
extra for my girl. I jumped out of my
truck out front full of excitement like I
hadn't just seen her hours ago. I had to
smile to myself at how much I felt like
a kid again.

Not that I ever really felt like a
kid before. But I imagine this is how
they felt on Xmas morning or in the
summer when school was out. I headed
for the counter where my order was
being packaged but was brought up
short in the middle of the room when
my body reacted.

What the fuck? I only felt that
tingle in my body when Dani was
close and she was at work on the other
side of town. I got my shit and was

about to call her to make sure she was okay. Couldn't think of any other reason for my sensing her this strong when she wasn't here. A quick scan of the room didn't turn up anything but it was as I was leaving that I heard her voice. She sounded...upset?

I walked around the huge potted plant that blocked a part of the room from view and my heart stopped. She was sitting at a table with some stuff shirt who seemed to be playing tug of war with her hand. My first instinct was to fuck everybody's shit up. I couldn't see through the red haze that covered my eyes as I set my body in fighter stance. But it was her next words that pulled me back from the brink just a little.

"Quit it Robert I thought you said you needed to talk."
"Get your fucking hands off her asshole." She almost jumped out of her chair when she heard my voice.
"Connor..."

"I'll deal with you later. You, hands, now." The little fuck released her hand and glowered at me when I stepped closer.

"Who is this person Danielle?" She looked at me as she stood and came over to my side.

"This is Connor Robert."

"Him? That's who you think you're going to marry? Your father will never allow you to marry this…this person."

Twenty five to life that's all I thought when I looked at him so I tamped down on the anger and ignored his dumb ass. As long as he wasn't touching her anymore the fucker could live. "I'll watch where I put my hands next time boy. I'm not too jazzed about motherfuckers touching what's mine. This is your one and only warning."

"Say goodbye Danielle." I didn't give her time as I pulled her out of the restaurant behind me.

"Connor I can explain."

"Don't talk to me right now you fucked up."

"I'm sorry I was just…"

"Shut your fucking mouth, I warned you."

I put her in the truck and belted her in. I was so furious it took me two tries to get that shit right.

"Connor…" She tried again but I was in no mood to hear her. For the first time in my life I came very close to striking a woman. Something I would never have imagined myself capable of.

"I told you to shut your fucking mouth." I dropped my hand quickly from her jaw; what the fuck was I doing? I didn't even realize I'd grabbed her face hard enough to leave impressions in her skin. I needed to calm the fuck down and quick. People were already looking as they passed by on the street.

No way was I going to be that fucking person. The asshole came to the doorway of the restaurant but had the good sense not to say a fucking word. I'm not sure I would've been able to walk away a second time. I gave him a look that had him taking a quick step back and had to be satisfied with that for now. I knew this fucker wasn't completely out of the picture. I hope he understood that today was his one and only shot though. Next time there will be blood.

I hopped into the driver's seat and sped off back to the site. She didn't say anything else but she was scared; good she needs to be.

I dropped the sacks of food on the table where my brothers usually gathered to have lunch when I got back to the site.

"I have something to take care of I won't be back for the rest of the day." Logan hawk eyed me as I turned to leave.

"Hold it, what's going on?"

"It's personal." I was barely holding onto my sanity by a thread here and I needed to be the fuck gone.
"Yeah and we're your family we don't hide shit from each other." The others sensing something was up stood around us.

"Is that Danielle in the truck?" Tyler looked in the direction of the truck and the others followed suit.

"What's going on Connor? Something happen to her?" Logan came to stand in front of me.
"Just let me deal with this shit I'll talk to you guys later."

"Connor you move from here we're gonna have problems. I know you brother I can read you like a book so I can see the fumes coming off you. Talk to me, we've been in tighter spots than this before and pulled through. Now what the fuck happened in the last half an hour to turn you into Killer?"

I don't think my brothers have ever called me that shit off the battlefield. It's the name they'd given me years ago because according to them when we were in the field my whole persona changed and I went into some other place in my head. They might not be too far off the mark with this one.

I wanted to commit murder. I can't believe she met this guy after I told her not to.
"What did she do bro?" Quinn watched me like he was ready to jump if I made the wrong move.

Fuck, I really didn't want to do this here and now. I just wanted to get her alone so I could deal with whatever the fuck that was. But I know these men. If they think I'm a danger to her they'll never stand the fuck down. "I caught her with her ex Quinn that's what the fuck she did."

"No way bro, she's in love with you anyone can see that shit."

"Well I saw them with my own two eyes Dev."

"Could you have misunderstood the situation?"

I made to head back to the truck but Logan got in my way again. "That's what I'm going to find out."

"Not like this you're not, you need to calm the fuck down before you do something we'll all regret."

"I'm cool."

"Zak get her out of there."

"Zak don't go near her; I said I'm fine, now either you trust me or you don't." I had to stare down each of my brothers to get them to back off. If I was freaking them out this much I can only imagine what she was feeling.

It took them a minute but eventually they stood down.

"Just stay cool brother we're here if you need us."

I nodded my head at Logan in understanding though I wasn't sure how cool I was gonna be dealing with this fucked up situation.

I walked away before they changed their minds. I knew that each of them had grown fond of her in a short space of time. They all knew what finding the one meant. We all knew this about each other.

It's not like we'd sat around and discussed the shit like a bunch of women. But we each knew how important it was. What it meant for one of us to bring a woman home. They'd all seen me struggle with whether or not to pursue her when she kept sending out signals. She was one of us now, but she'd fucked up. Now I have to go see just how much.

Back in the truck I didn't say anything to her as I started it and drove off. I didn't talk to her the whole way home, just concentrated on driving and trying to get a handle on the anger that was burning in my gut. I could see that she was nervous as I drove through the gates of home but I didn't care. I didn't try to reassure her when she looked at me with pleading eyes. A deal's a deal.

With me there was no room for screw-ups. Two things, I'd asked her for two fucking things and we weren't even in a month yet and she pulls this shit.

"Get inside." She jumped out of the truck and ran to the house. I wasn't quite sure what I intended to do to her, I just knew that she'd been warned. The memory of his hands on her burned into my brain as I got out and followed her. She stood in the middle of the kitchen wringing her hands nervously as I walked in. I just stood there and looked at her for what felt like hours as I tried to calm myself down.

"Come here." She did the wrong thing then when she shook her head and backed away from me.
"Don't fucking run from me Danielle I said come here."
"No Connor please you're scaring me."
"Come…here."

She still didn't move towards me and that just pissed me off farther. Before I could think better of it I was removing my belt and she took off running. "Don't make me come after you baby." I followed her retreating form out of the kitchen, anger burning in my gut. My woman fucking ran from me.

"Connor quit it I didn't do anything." She was crying and pleading as she tried to escape me. I caught up with her on the stairs and grabbed her arm, pulling her around. I don't think I've ever been that mad in my fucking life. She'd run from me like I was some kind of fucking monster. This on top of what I'd just seen was almost too much for me to take.

"Where in the fuck are you going?" She kept her eyes on the leather belt in my hand.
"What did I tell you about seeing him?" I pulled her forward and glared into her face. I didn't care that her eyes

were filled with terror. In that moment I didn't give a fuck about anything but getting the picture of the two of them together out of my head.

"I wasn't seeing him he called and said he wanted to talk I felt, I felt..."
"You felt what Danielle, what the fuck did you feel?" I shook her when she didn't say anything more.

"I just wanted to keep the peace. I felt I owed him an explanation after the way I'd just broken things off. Someone told him about us. I was just trying to keep things calm."
"That's all bullshit. I told you to stay away from that fuck and you let him put his hands on you?"

"He didn't..."
"I saw him with his fucking hands on you don't lie to me."
"Please I didn't mean anything by it."
"I've never hit a woman in my life but right now I could smack the shit out of

you. I don't know what the fuck to do with this."

"You don't have to do anything because nothing happened." Her body was trembling in my hands and I found myself in the precarious position of wanting to reassure her and tan her ass at the same time. I looked at her and some of her fear finally penetrated. I'd never wanted to see that look on her face. Never wanted to be the one to put it on any woman's face. And especially not the one I was supposed to love above all others.

"This is fucked. Do you know how close I came to hitting you? I refuse to let you destroy me. I've spent my whole life trying not to be this person and in one day look at what the fuck you brought me to. Was it worth it to see him huh?"
She didn't answer me just hung her head and cried. "Connor I'm sorry I didn't think…please."

"Look I'm the fuck out of here, I think I need to get the fuck away from you right now."

"No Connor, please I'm sorry it won't happen again I'm sorry." She grabbed onto me as I turned to head back down the stairs.

My brothers were right I needed to calm the fuck down before I did something I'd regret. With this much anger and heat I'd only end up doing more damage than good anyway. I felt empty as fuck. Disappointed, disillusioned, all the things I've been trying to avoid my whole fucking life when it came to this relationship bullshit.

"Get off of me, I don't know what to believe right now. You told me you understood you fucking lied; you do not want to fuck with me on this shit."

My head was too hot; I knew that was a dangerous thing for her. Knew that in the next few minutes I could

174 | JORDAN SILVER

start down a road that might taint our relationship forever. I was so fucking pissed right then though that it almost didn't matter. This is the reason I'd made her swear that she understood. The memory of that asshole's hands on her kept playing over and over in my head.

She cried harder and held onto me instead of trying to get away like she had been. I looked down at her, her tearstained face was now even more afraid than before. Her eyes wide with fear, not of my belt but of me walking away. I couldn't say anything to her for the longest time, couldn't do anything but just look at her. I was trying to come to terms with what I'd almost done; the weight of the belt in my hand was almost sickening.

Looking into her eyes seeing the agony there was like a bucket of cold water in my face. I grabbed her neck and pulled her forward into my chest.

"Stop crying I'm not gonna hurt you I will never hurt you okay."
"But you're gonna leave me." She cried harder and grabbed onto me with both hands as though she could keep me there by sheer will alone.

I hugged her closer and took a deep breath. I didn't know what the fuck I wanted to do; this was new territory for me. I've never felt the urge to fight over a woman, never wanted to slap the shit out of one either.

For all I know it could've been as innocent as she said but the fact still remained that she'd gone behind my back and did the one thing I'd asked her not to. That shit stuck in my craw, if I couldn't trust her then there was nothing. The thought fucking gutted me.

"Look at me." She turned her face up to me, and I studied her. I had to get her to understand so that this would never happen again. I never wanted to reach this point ever again in my life. I have no problem spanking her ass this is not about that. But I would be damned if I'm going to raise my hand to her when I was this angry. I knew that I could really hurt her if I did that shit. So how do I get past this? How do I work this so we never end up here again?

"You fucked up royally baby, this is not something I take lightly. I told you I didn't want you anywhere near him again. I laid my cards on the table there was no room for misunderstanding. You fucking disrespected me so you know what. Before I do something that I'll regret I think it best that I stay the fuck away from you for the next little while."

"Where are you going?" She tried running after me as I turned to walk away.
"I have to get back to the job site."
"Can't you stay and talk to me?"

"No Danielle, I have nothing more to say. Why don't you figure out what you want? I'm done, what you almost caused me to do is not something I can just shove under the rug. You have to decide if you can live with what I want from you, if you can't then I'll help you move your shit when I get back."

I felt sick when I got back in my truck and headed back to work. I wanted to go hunt that fucker down and put my hand through his face after all, but this wasn't about him. She's the one who fucked up, he has no loyalty to me she's supposed to. Besides if I put my hands on that fucker he'd end up dead.

I wasn't too worried about that crack he'd made about her father. I wasn't marrying him if he couldn't accept me then fuck him too. Maybe it was a good thing that this had happened now, when we were still fresh, still new. I guess I should feel some relief that I'd been able to pull

178 | JORDAN SILVER

back and not go through with it. But all I felt was drained.

I had a lot of shit to think about in the next few hours before I went back to her. I wasn't ready to try to understand her reasoning, as fat as I'm concerned she had none. Fuck. If we get past this I'm going to drive this shit home once and for all because I'm never going there again.

Chapter 11

My brothers eyed me the rest of the day like a ticking time bomb about to detonate. I ignored them too and took out my frustration on hammer and nails. Each time I tried to make sense of the situation I came up empty. I was trying like hell to get a handle on my anger but I kept coming back to one thing. She'd disobeyed. It wasn't like there was room for misinterpretation. I don't want you anywhere near him again is as plain as it gets as far as I'm concerned.

I guess I wasn't doing a very good job of containing my anger because the others kept their distance though I could sense their eyes on me every once in a while. I ignored them and did my thing. I had to put it away for now to clear my head. I wasn't getting anywhere going round and round in my head. I was still pissed, nothing had changed there.

Of course Logan was the one to approach me a little while later.
"So how did it go brother?"
"We're good."
"Don't feed me that bullshit bro, talk."
"She fucked up big time Lo. I don't even know what to do with this shit. I told her to stay the fuck away from this guy and what does she do?"

"I'm sure she didn't mean anything by it. You can't make me believe that she has any interest in this guy. We've all seen her with you Connor, she lights the fuck up when you're around. And when you're not looking she fucking eats you alive with her eyes bro."

By now the others had joined us and of course I had to hear their input as well. Everyone had pretty much the same take. Dani would never cheat on me. That wasn't necessarily my

problem the problem was she
disobeyed.

"Guys you know what this is
about, I can't have her being
disobedient. What if some shit happens
and she doesn't listen and gets hurt?"
"You're thinking like a SEAL bro…"
"I am a fucking SEAL Zak."
"You know what I mean. This is
civilian life they don't think the way
we do she doesn't see it as being
disobedient she's just you know…"

"Did she tell you why she was
with him?" Ty was usually the more
silent of the group except when it
comes to food. He especially steered
away from talks about relationships.
That's why it was so surprising that
he'd been the one hounding me about
going after Danielle. So I know out of
everyone he would stand for her.

"Yeah, something about
explaining things to him. Someone
told him about us and I guess she
never told him why she broke up with

him months ago and he wanted to know."

"That seems reasonable to me, and they were in a public place bro, it's not like she met him at a hotel or some shit."

"I know that Quinn but you're all missing the point, I told her not to do it. If I tell my woman not to do something I expect her to follow orders."

"Bro do you hear yourself? This is not the battlefield."

"You think so Cord? It's the toughest one yet bro. Wait until it's your turn and we'll see how the rest of you handle your shit."

I went back to work, done with the conversation. I didn't expect anyone to understand why I felt the way I did. As close as we all were there were some things that I'd never shared with my brothers, just as I'm sure there were some things they kept close to the vest as well.

I'd grown up hard and rough in one of the toughest inner cities of the nation. Gang bangers and turf wars were an everyday thing. Going to school was like walking through a minefield most days but that was outside. It's what went on inside behind closed doors that scarred me for life. A disinterested mother and an alcoholic abusive stepfather who thought it was fun to use me as an ashtray on a good day and a football on the others.

By the time I was thirteen I'd suffered more broken bones and black eyes than a professional prizefighter but still no one stepped in. No one seemed to notice the scrawny little kid who was just drifting away right before their very eyes. Worse than the beatings and the abuse though was the way those two treated each other. Although they were my worst nightmare they were all I had and the screaming and fighting between those two made me sick with fear.

If anything happened what would happen to me? Where would I end up? I used to count down the years until it was time to get out. I'd set my sights on the service as my fastest way out; that had been my goal. But in the meantime I had to endure them; it was from them I learned my first distrust of the human race. I saw the infidelity and the beatings, the name-calling and the degradation.

I promised myself then that I would never hit a woman. That I would never find myself in a relationship with such contention. In my head I'd decided that the woman I met and fell in love with some day would be perfect, we'd never fight, never argue. As a grown man I knew that was just a pipe dream but I still didn't want any of that shit in my life. What Danielle did today took me back to a dark place that I thought I'd escaped from, a place I never wanted to revisit again in this lifetime.

By the time I reached the house that evening I still wasn't any closer to knowing what the fuck I wanted to do about the situation. She was in the kitchen when I walked in but I just walked right by her and up the stairs to the shower. I had my head buried under the water's spray when I felt arms wrap around me from behind.

I didn't turn, not even when she laid her head on my back. I'd spent the last half hour questioning whether or not I could live without this. Whether I could go the rest of my life without her in it. That's how scared this shit had made me. I would rather spend the rest of my life alone than to relive my past. But I knew I could never live without her now. I'd had her; her sweetness had seeped into me and wrapped me up tight. I'd fucking die without her.

I pulled her around in front of me pushing her hair back so I could see her face. Her red puffy eyes told me

she'd spent the afternoon crying. I
pulled her to me and kissed her hard
holding her as close as I could before
pushing her away again. We studied
each other for the longest time without
saying a word.

"You do this shit to me again I'll
fucking kill you Danielle and be done
with it. Do you understand me?" I
shook her for emphasis as her eyes
filled up with tears. Dragging her
against me I took her mouth hard
lifting her so she straddled my hips.
"Put me inside you." Her hand reached
between us and fed my cock into her
pussy.

"Now fuck me like you're sorry."
She slid up and down the length of my
cock. It was then I realized how long
my cock really was as she lifted herself
on and off of it. When it bent for the
third time I took her down to the
bottom of the shower and fucked into
her hard.

"This is your punishment." I pounded into her as the water washed over us. I fucked her hard and deep working off all the fucking anger that was still burning inside. When I couldn't get the friction I needed because of the hard surface beneath her I pulled her up and with her pussy still locked around my dick headed out of the shower. I barely ran a towel over us before throwing it to the floor and heading for the bed.

I didn't talk to her. There were no soft words and touches. I knew damn well I was using my dick to punish her ass and she knew that shit too. I held her eyes with mine as I plunged into her over and over again. Lifting her legs all the way up and out, I held her ankles open wide and watched as my cock sliced into her pink swollen pussy.

"Play with your clit." Her fingers came down to touch her clit as I fucked her deep. Bending over double I took her nipple into my mouth and sucked hard before biting into it hard enough to make her scream. She came all over my cock and went wild. Fuck yeah baby. I pounded even harder trying to erase the anger, trying to exorcise it inside her.

"Connor…" She tried to ease off my dick by sliding up the bed but I followed. "Stay." I pulled her back onto my cock hard as fuck. Dropping her legs I stopped moving inside her and wrapped my hand around her throat. "Look at me. Who do you belong to?"
"You Connor, please…" She started crying again but fuck that, she fucked up she wasn't getting off that fucking easy.

"That's right, this is mine." I thrust into her hard once. "You are mine, all of you. Turn over." I pulled my cock out and waited. She got up on her hands and knees and I slipped my dick back into her. Grabbing a fistful of her hair I fucked into her trying to release the anger and the pain.

I wasn't careful with her this time like I usually am. Instead I fucked her the way I've always wanted to. I bit into the skin between her neck and shoulder as I held her hair tight and pounded into her, going deep. She begged me not to hurt her pussy anymore but I didn't stop. I wanted her to feel pain, the same way she'd made me fucking bleed.

"Next time I won't hold back. Next time I will whip your ass black and blue. Give me your fucking tongue." She turned her head and fed me her tongue as I lifted her almost straight with her back to y chest. My cock pounded up into her hard and fast until I came hard and long with an animalistic growl.

She dropped onto the bed holding her hurt pussy. "That little stunt you pulled just cost you your fucking freedom." I went back to the bathroom to finish cleaning up. My head was still hot but not as fucked up as it was earlier. I now find myself in the position of having to deal with her in a way I never would've expected.

She's my little southern belle, she's soft and sweet and should be treated like the princess she is. But now there's going to be another element added. All the shit I'd held off from doing to and with her because I thought she was too soft was now on the fucking table. She'd unleashed the bastard in me, now she could deal with that shit.

She was sitting on the side of the bed looking like she'd just come through a storm. I didn't have time for that shit either, I'd be fucked if she was gonna get away with disobeying me. "Let's eat." I walked out of the room wearing my jeans and nothing else. I was fucking starved suddenly. She'd made a roast and potatoes.

I set the table and waited for her to come down. She wasn't walking too straight when she finally showed up but I didn't have time to care about that shit either. She sat and played with her food until that shit got on my nerves. "Eat." She looked up at me like I was a stranger; she better believe she'd never seen this motherfucker before. I looked at her and down at her fork until she picked that shit up and started eating. There was nothing said for a good five minutes. I was too busy slicing into my meat and imagining that fucker's face.

"Connor."

"What is it?" I didn't even bother to look at her.

"I'm sorry."

"Yeah well you should be." That was the end of that. We went back to eating in silence.

Chapter 12

We were finally getting somewhere with the fuckery that was going on in the town. It wasn't much but it was a start. The cigarette brand that we'd found was only sold in one town remotely close to Briarwood so that pinned it down. The town of Blue Fin was an affluential area with industry big wigs and those secretive motherfuckers that owned everything. The ones you never heard shit about.

We couldn't exactly go around asking questions in a place like that so we had to try piecing everything together behind the scenes. Old man Connelly didn't know of any connections between the two towns but promised to do some digging on the sly. There was no way to keep him from doing that shit so all we could do was make sure he was being careful.

We still hadn't been able to set up surveillance because there was no good time to do shit the way it would do the most good. But Logan said he was working on it. That was his shit so we left him to it. We did put ears down there though which so far hadn't picked up anything useful. Either they had a routine as to when they visited the pier or they weren't meeting in the same spot anymore. And since there hadn't been any more cigarette butts we were more inclined to believe they hadn't been back since. We'd left a few from the last time so there wouldn't be any suspicions, just in case the fuckers were that diligent. Then again if they were they wouldn't have left them in the first place.

At least the nights out got me out of the house and away from Danielle's sulking ass. She usually spent the time on the phone with her girls, probably discussing what a dick I am. I give a fuck.

For two weeks I stayed on her ass. I drove her to and from work and when it was my turn to do a lunch run I took her lunch. My brothers did it the other days. They hadn't said anything more about the situation and I didn't bring it up. What was there to say?

They still had dinner with us most nights and I'm sure they could sense the tension in the air. The only time there wasn't tension is when I was fucking her. Then there was a whole other kind of tension. I wasn't as mad at her as before but I was still pissed that she'd done that shit.

She was into walking around me like she expected me to lose my shit any second and that was beginning to wear on my nerves too. She didn't seem to understand I was just waiting for her to get what she'd fucking done wrong. She'd said sorry a million times but I still don't think she understood how serious this shit was to me. Or what the fuck it is she was supposed to be sorry for.

To her it might've been an innocent meeting to clear the air as she'd claimed. To me it was my woman disobeying me. And not just disobeying me but doing it with the fucker she'd once been engaged to, the only other man to have her. Maybe I'm wrong, maybe this shit shouldn't mean anything, but fuck it meant something to me. I didn't even want the fucker breathing farther more being in the same room as her.

We were sitting at the dinner table once more. She'd tried playing the 'I'll eat later' card a few nights ago and I'd nipped that shit in the bud. I'm sure she thinks I'm being too hard on her but she has no idea. I'm trying to avoid any future fuck ups of this magnitude because there's no guarantee I'll be able to hold back if there is a next time. She lifted her fork to her mouth and I noticed her bare hand and remembered something important that I'd forgotten to take care of.

"Tomorrow we're going shopping." She picked her head up and looked at me. She was probably wondering if all was forgiven since this was the first time I'd initiated a conversation since that bullshit happened. Like I said the only time I said anything to my woman in two weeks is when I was buried balls deep inside her. And then it was usually only to remind her who the fuck she belonged to. She's been on a steady diet of that shit.

"I promised Candy and Gabriella…" I cut her off before she went any farther.
"Don't care babe. Tomorrow, you and me." I got up from the table and walked to the sink. When I turned around she was still pouting. "I guess you didn't hear me when I said your little stunt cost you your freedom. Well let me spell that shit out for you again. You don't do anything without me telling you it's okay. Nothing Danielle, and fix your fucking face."

"I can't believe you're really being this way over one stupid mistake. A mistake that wasn't even…" She cut herself off this time and kept her head down.

"Wasn't even what? A mistake? Is that what you were about to say?" I walked over and grabbed her chin lifting her face to mine. "That's where you're wrong, and that's the fucking problem. You don't see it as a mistake you don't see what you did wrong. Until you do we'll never get back to where we were." I dropped her chin and walked away. She followed behind me in a huff. "Connor we can't go on like this, this is crazy. It's been two weeks of the silent treatment and the cold shoulder. I'm not accustomed to living like this it's not fair."

"Oh I see, it's all about Danielle, forget the fact that you fucked up. I should cater to your spoilt ass because it's what you're accustomed to." She folded her arms and her little face became mutinous. She looked like she'd like nothing better than to belt me one. It was almost laughable but I wouldn't give her even that. She had to earn my smiles again fuck that.

"I just think you're taking it too far Connor. For heaven's sake you brushed off dinner with my parents because of this." She's right, I had. When her mom had finally called with arrangements for dinner I'd told her I couldn't make it but maybe her daughter could. I'd even dropped her there and picked her up. She'd been miserable as fuck but I had no intentions on playing pretend for her family. Not now not ever.

"You should've told them the truth as to why. If your mom had asked me I would've told her. And if your father is any kind of a man he'd understand where I'm coming from. On the other hand if he doesn't I don't really give a fuck about that either. You're my woman, they're my rules, learn to live with it."

I turned again and headed up the stairs, I was done with the whole fucking situation. She was never going to get this shit. How do you make your woman understand that you needed her to do the shit you say because you don't want to hurt her? Because you're afraid that if she slips up again you might lose your shit and do something that you know you shouldn't?

I heard the TV come on downstairs as I lay across the bed to read. I'll let her have her little snit before I was ready for her ass. It's probably not very nice of me to admit but I enjoyed making her body sing for mine even though she was pissed at me. No matter how mad she was as soon as we got into bed and I turned to her she had no defenses against me.

Tonight I had something new for my little wife to be. She's been fucked more in the past two weeks than all the others combined. From the time I got her in the door in the evenings I was in her. That's because I spent most of the day thinking about this shit, so by that time I needed to work it off.

At night as soon as dinner was over it was on again. She didn't have time for anything else since I was basically fucking her into submission. She hasn't complained as yet, not since that first night when she said I hurt her pussy. I guess she was getting used to it.

I think the nights we went patrolling the boardwalk were the only peaceful ones she had, until I came home and climbed into bed with her. The funny thing is though, that she always turns to me in the night. Those first few nights I tried sleeping with my back to her. Within an hour of her falling asleep she'd be pressed up to my back with her nose in my spine. Of course me being the fucking sap that I am I usually rolled over and held her. That's the only time I let my guard down and was sweet to her. When she was asleep.

I gave it another hour before calling her up the stairs. "Danielle get up here." I heard the TV turn off and not a minute later her feet on the stairs. She knew better than to make me wait, we'd already played that game. It had taken her pussy a good day to get over the pounding she'd endured over that debacle. Even if she wasn't getting what it was I needed her to get, she was learning in a roundabout way what she had to look forward to if she fucked with me.

"Come here. Lose the clothes on your way." I was already naked, reclining back against the pillows with my dick in hand. I stroked slowly up and down as I watched her get undressed. Even that was done the way I'd taught her that I liked, slow and precise. She kept her eyes on mine the whole time until she was standing there before me bare.

"Touch yourself." I heard the sharp intake of breath before she pinked up. But her hands moved to obey me. "Slowly." She touched her nipples first, pulling and twisting on them until they were pointed and swollen. Her hands moved down her stomach nice and slow until she reached her sweet snatch.

She used her middle finger to rub against her clit back and forth. "Now go inside." Two fingers went up and inside her as that one hand stayed on her nipple. "Fuck yourself on your fingers." I had to ease up on stroking my meat because what she was doing to herself was really getting to me. Her body still captivates me, still makes me want to howl at the fucking moon. Even with my mad.

"Suck your pussy from your fingers and then come here." She pulled out the two fingers pushing them into her mouth and licking them clean. When she was done she walked over to the bed where I was waiting for her. "Climb up." I helped her up and over my face sitting her pussy on my tongue.

"Ooh." She was already moving on my tongue; she did like having her pussy eaten. I feasted on her until my mouth was full of her taste. But that's not what this was about. I eased her off my face and sat her on my chest before reaching over to the night table. Holding her eyes captive I reached around behind her. "Lift up." She lifted just a little so I could reach her ass to oil it up for what was to come. After I'd oiled her up nicely I passed her the tube. "Grease my cock."

She bit her bottom lip as she squeezed some into her hand and rubbed them together. Then she massaged it into my cock nice and slow. I could see her nervousness in the erratic beat of her pulse. Pulling her lips down to mine I kissed her nice and slow letting her taste her pussy on my tongue.

"Sit up. Look at my cock." I held my cock at the base. It was long thick and angry looking. She swallowed hard as she knew that every last inch was going into her ass. Eleven inches of steel, she could barely handle me in her pussy; let's see how she does with her ass. "Hold yourself up for me." She lifted up a little and looked down between her legs at where I was rubbing my bulbous cockhead back and forth from her pussy to her ass. On each third slide I'd slip just the tip inside her wet pussy before pulling back.

"Lean over baby. Not that much. Right there." I took her nipple into my mouth and sucked as I eased my cock inside her ass slowly, inch by inch until there was about three inches inside her. I could feel her body getting ready to tense up so I held still and concentrated on her tits. Her hands gripped the headboard as I pushed another inch inside and she hissed.

"Relax because you're taking all of me. Mouth." She leaned down and fed me her tongue as I slipped farther inside her ass and started to thrust. I used short strokes at first until she was seated completely on my cock. I fingered her clit with my thumb making it nice and wet before finger fucking her with it.

"Ride." She had one of those hurt so good looks on her face as she learned the ins and outs of having a stiff cock in her ass for the first time. I helped her out with a hand on her hip guiding her up and down until she got the hang of it and took over.

She was soon riding my cock and grinding down on the thumb in her pussy. "Feels good?" She nodded her head yes as she picked up speed. "Uh huh." Her tits bounced as she rode me easier and easier. I pulled my thumb out and sat up so I could tongue and suck her nipples, first one then the other.

When they were nice and plump I grabbed two fistfuls of her hair and brought her mouth to mine. "Kiss me." Our mouths fought for dominance until I nipped her lip and won the war. Taking her to her back I drove into her harder and deeper testing the waters so to speak. She didn't cry out for pain or at least the little peep she made wasn't cause for concern so I kept going. With her legs over my arms I straightened my legs, and planting my toes into the mattress fucked into her ass straight. She bucked and hissed as my groin rubbed against her clit with each forward stroke.

"I'm cumming Connor." I took her mouth again licking her lips before pushing my tongue inside. She sucked me into her ass and mouth simultaneously as her pussy juices gushed onto my lower stomach. I wasn't too far behind as the contractions of her ass soon had me spewing inside her.

I came with a loud harsh groan before pulling out and back, diving into her pussy with my tongue. I licked up all her spilt sweetness until there was none left. "Stay where you are, just as you are." Her legs were still up and open leaving her pussy well exposed.

I made fast work of cleaning my cock in the bathroom before going back to her, my cock hard and throbbing. The greedy fuck never gets enough of his girl. She watched me as I came towards the bed stroking my hardness. Climbing up between her thighs I teased her pussy with my cock.

Up, down, and back again until she writhed and begged me for it. "Please Connor." She was hot and panting for my dick, just the way I like her. "Please what Danielle?" I tapped her clit with my heavy pre cum covered cockhead. "Oooh...make love to me please." Not good enough. I went back to teasing her only this time

I fed her two inches on each downward slide before pulling out again. "You want me to make love to you, or fuck the shit out of you?"

She pinked up and bit her lip but when I slipped my tip inside she arched and gave me what I wanted. "Fuck me, please Connor, just fuck me." I pulled back and slammed home hard making her scream. Laying my body flat against hers with her hands clasped in mine over her head I ground my cock into her at an angle.

I searched for and found that little patch inside her that makes her sing and rubbed my cockhead against it. She creamed my cock and bucked beneath me, her head raised so she could sink her teeth into my neck. I never stopped fucking into her even when her pussy clamped down and pulsed around me. "Fuck yeah take my cock baby."

"Too much Connor, it's too much…" I attacked her nipple with my teeth as her over sensitive skin heated up beneath me. I used my whole body to tease her. Rubbing my groin into her clit, my arm brushed against her other nipple. There wasn't a part of her that wasn't on fire.

Now I want her mind. "You loved getting your ass fucked didn't you Danielle? My sweet little Georgia peach, tell me." I reared up and looked down at her as I stroked into her slower this time, giving her room to talk. She was too far-gone, her body wild and uninhibited beneath the onslaught of my cock. I jabbed her with my cock hard to get her attention.

"Answer me or I'll stop." She turned glazed eyes up to me as her fingers tightened around mine. "You want me to stop?"
"No no don't stop…YES I loved having you there." I'll let her get away with that one for now. I lifted her legs high and wide for deeper penetration then bent over her so I could whisper in her ear. "I've changed my mind

about waiting. Since you want to be disobedient we'll get started on my son now." I pulled back to catch the look of surprise on her face. "I will fuck you everyday until I know he's in you. Then and only then Danielle will I stop being this fucking pissed. Tell me you want my son."

"I do…I…Connor." I guess she did like the idea because she came hard as fuck on my cock.

Chapter 13

The next day we got up and dressed to go on our little shopping trip. She had no idea where we were off to and I didn't answer her any of the ten times she asked over breakfast. Things were a little less tense between us today. After I'd made up in my mind to fuck my son into her my mind had finally found peace. The idea made me hard just thinking about it. She wasn't going anywhere no matter what so there was no point in prolonging the issue. Also with my kind in her, that should send the message to other assholes to back the fuck off.

I didn't even know where Robert the fuck lived. I've never seen him around and I thought it best not to get that information less I lose my shit in the middle of the night and go off his ass for being stupid. "Come here baby." I pushed back my chair so she could come sit in my lap. She had the biggest fucking smile on her face as she put her arm around my neck.

I missed this shit, missed the easiness between us. If she didn't get it by now she never would. But somehow I'm sure she won't ever be making that mistake again anytime soon if ever. She didn't wait for me to ask for her mouth, she took the initiative and planted one on me.

I had her straddling me with her jeans undone in five seconds flat. "Take these off." I helped her wrestle out her jeans and threw them to the floor before unzipping and releasing my cock. She sat back in my lap and I pushed her shirt and bra up and out of the way.

The guys knew not to show their faces over here on a weekend morning until much later but I'd told them last night I had to make a run this morning so they had to scrounge for breakfast themselves. There was a lot of grumbling and complaining especially from Ty but whatever.

I sucked her nipple into my mouth and rubbed my cock on her clit, clit fucking her with just the swollen head. She made those little hissing noises she makes when her pussy needs me so I didn't make her wait too long before lifting her far enough to seat her on my cock and pull her down all the way until her ass was touching my thighs.

"Tongue." She gave me her mouth as she rode up and down on my cock with my hands on her ass moving her just how I wanted her. "Squeeze my cock babe." She did the flexing exercises I'd taught her and I almost bit off her tongue. Getting to my feet I laid her back across the table pushing the dishes and shit to the side so I could fuck into her the way I needed to.

Spreading her open I looked down between us where my cock was sawing into her long and deep. I thumbed her clit making it even puffier as her hot pussy sucked my cock in like she was starved for it. "Cum baby." I took her nipple again and ground into her hitting her sweet spot until she screamed into my mouth.

I emptied inside her before pulling out and retaking my seat. "Clean me off babe." She dropped to her knees and took my cock into her mouth licking her pussy juice from my cock and nuts until I was semi hard again. "You might as well finish him off now. " She got to work deep throating my shit until I came a long time later down her throat.

When we were done fucking around I took her back upstairs and cleaned us both up before going about the shit I had to do.

I had her on the back of bike as we headed out of town, what I was looking for wasn't going to be here I'm sure. We talked and laughed on the way and I felt the stress ease with each mile that went by. She held me a little tighter around the middle as we sped along and rested her head on my back. Every once in a while she'd squeeze me and I'd smile behind the screen of my helmet. I know what that shit was about. She'd been fucked hard, she'd been introduced to new kink and she liked that shit.

Her mouth opened wide when we got off the bike in the parking lot of one of the nation's most exclusive jeweler. "Let's go." I had to practically drag her along behind me. She was probably wondering what an ex SEAL could possibly afford in a place like this. I'm sure the asshole hadn't gotten her a ring here. Yes I had to top his shit. I'd never seen her ring come to think of it. "Who chose your last ring?" She got a very uncomfortable look on her face so I took it between my hands and looked into her eyes. "We're all good baby just answer the question."

"He did." She didn't want to have this conversation at all and neither did I but I needed to top this motherfucker in every way. I hadn't forgotten that crack he'd made about her father not allowing her to marry someone like me. Like I was some sort of fucking mutt. "How many carats?" She looked up at me as if about to argue.

Oh yeah, I'm well aware of the way the human mind works. It's how I profiled the assholes we hunted in the Navy. How I gauged their next move so I could take them the fuck out. There's never gonna be a day that she looks down at her finger and think his was bigger or better, fuck that. And since this one was never coming off her finger it had to be her favorite. "Two and a half."

"Fine, your choice, four and a half and up." She pulled back on my hand. And started to shake her head. She also looked nervous as fuck. "Don't worry Danielle, you won't break me if you buy a ring that you like. I told you before I've been investing my money for years. Never had anything to spend the shit on before. I want you to have the shit you want, something you and your girls can coo over. You got me?" She still wasn't too convinced but at least she wasn't looking like she was ready to bolt any second.

Inside the store the saleslady came over all smiles and offered her assistance. I stood back and watched the action as they went through tray after tray of rings. I read her body language, I know my woman so I knew the minute she saw THE one. I wasn't surprised when she kept going though. All I did was shake my head as I stood off to the side out of their way but I kept my eye on it for her. Two hours later she chose some bullshit ring that was about half the size of what I'd told her. She'd looked back at that damn ring sneakily of course, about every ten minutes or less.

"So you like this one?" The saleslady held up the bullshit ring and my girl looked back at me. I'm sure the shit had to be at least twenty-five grand. Harry didn't do shit for much less. I walked over to the case where the ring she'd fallen in love with sat and pointed. "We'll take this one."

"Connor..."
"Quiet." The saleslady came over and removed the tray and started spouting off specs. Something about cushion cut whatever. I had no fucking idea and could care less. It was five carats and it's the one she wanted that was good enough for me. She tried to argue with me but I just gave her a look. "This the

one you like Dani? Tell me the truth."
She nodded shyly and hung her head.

"Babe what did I tell you before
we came in here? See this is why
you're gonna stay in trouble you don't
listen for shit." I said that shit out of
earshot of the others in the store. I
wasn't about embarrassing my woman
in public, but damn her head is hard as
fuck.

"You can ring that up ma'am."
I took it out of the box as soon as the
transaction was over and slid it onto
her finger.
"This stays, always. It doesn't come
off for any reason." She stared at that
shit until I lifted her mouth and kissed
her right there in the middle of the
store. And that easily I felt the last of
the bitterness fall away. Don't be
fooled, I'm still waiting for her to get
what the fuck she did wrong the only
difference is now I'm willing to wait
for her to get that shit. It's the only
way she won't fuck up again.

We were one step closer to complete ownership. All that was left was the wedding which I'm gonna get on as soon as fucking possible. Her mom had made noises about these things taking time to plan but I'm giving them three months tops and even that was pushing it.

We walked around for a few but I could tell she was anxious to get back. Probably needed to call her girls and talk about her new haul. "Can I go show mama?" See that's a sure sign that my girl had got the right fucking ring. She couldn't wait to show that shit off and fuck yes I was pleased as shit. "We can do whatever you want babe." Her sweet smile was back in full force and I realized how much I'd missed that shit. Hopefully for the next little while there wouldn't be any fuck ups to send me off my ass again.

After we swung by her family's estate so her mom could gush over her ring and her dad could finally size me up it was back to the compound to my nosy ass brothers. Her old man hadn't been what I'd expected though. He'd asked me into his library while the women went on and on about weddings and shit. I was ready for anything he had to throw at me. After the last couple weeks there wasn't anything that was going to get in the way of me holding onto what the fuck was mine.

"Connor I have to admit that when my wife first told me about you and my daughter I had my doubts. You have to understand that little girl out there is my one and only offspring so it wouldn't have mattered who you were I would've felt the same. I'm sure you know she was engaged for a little while to someone else?" He looked at me through the cigar smoke and I stared back at him.

"Yep." He laughed at my stance before taking a seat behind the sea of wood that he called a desk.
"Stand down soldier I'm not about to start anything those two out there would have my guts for garters if I did. I just wanted to give you my blessing. My little girl is as happy as I've ever seen her and that's all that matters to me. With that said you hurt my baby and I'll skin you alive."

"She's my baby now sir so you have no worries." I relaxed my shoulders a little since it wasn't looking like he was going to start shit. We kicked around old army and navy tales killing time until the women were done doing whatever the hell they were doing and joined us. My girl came over to me and wrapped her arms around me. "Daddy you haven't been giving my guy a hard time have you?" I squeezed her shoulders and kissed her hair to let her know that it was all good.

"We have to get going my brothers will be waiting for us." I wasn't exactly uncomfortable but I didn't want to hang around. He seemed cool enough but this shit was weird. I was fucking his daughter and he knew it. Not sure I could be as cool about that shit as he seemed to be.

"We're having all boys." I told her that shit as soon as we were outside.

"What? Why?" She stopped short and looked at me like I had two fucking heads.

"Not up for debate babe, just make that shit happen."

"Uh Connor I'm pretty sure that's on you."

     "Yeah but females be pulling a fast one and putting in a good word for what they want, kind of a Blitzkrieg move. None of that sneaky shit Danielle. If you want your man to have a peace of mind no girls." She thought that shit was funny but I was dead serious. I have no problem violating Danielle's sweet as fuck body but fuck. I can't think about this shit it will make me lose my fucking nut.

Chapter 14

After that it was back home. Where we were now, surrounded by my brothers. All in all the day had turned out just fine. My woman was happy and I no longer felt like killing a motherfucker. I couldn't wait to get her alone to seal the deal but the boys had other ideas.

"We need to go celebrate you two." Logan brought up the idea of going out for drinks and dancing later and since she seemed excited by the idea I went along with it. I'm not much for that shit but I can't keep her locked away behind stonewalls forever. She called up some of her girls at my request and we headed for the showers after the others left.

Seeing my seal of ownership on her hand did something crazy to me. She was shampooing her hair when the light caught that shit just right and my cock grew stiff. I barely let her get the soap out of her hair before I was covering her mouth with mine, backing her up to the wall. "Wrap your legs around me." She did as I asked and I just pushed my finger inside her to test her wetness. She sucked it in and pushed so I pulled it out and sank my cock inside her instead.

"I'm gonna fuck you hard and rough baby hold on." I pounded into her pinning her to the wall with my thrusts. Our mouths fused together as I fed her my tongue before taking hers into my mouth. Her pussy was tight and needy around my length as she tried her best to keep up. I wanted to fuck every inch of her. Mark her in more ways than one. The need to stake my claim completely was too much to ignore. We had a few hours before it was time to leave hopefully that would be enough.

I almost cancelled the night but she pouted, she was all excited to show off her ring and shit. I don't know how she was walking after the freaky shit I'd just done to her but she was. I could go another few hours but I guess I could hold my shit until we got home later.

"Um babe I like that shit." She had on low rider jeans and a satin halter-top that matched her green eyes and heels that were a mile high. I think she was trying to match me in height with those shits. She did some wild shit with her hair that had curls falling down her back and all I could think of was grabbing fistfuls of that shit while I hit her pussy from behind. Damn I've become a fiend.

The guys were waiting for us when we stepped outside all of us looking like we were in uniform. Jeans, Henley, and leather jackets with shit kickers. No wonder people think we're a gang.

I made sure she was fine on the back of my ride in those fuck me heels and we headed out.

The place we'd chosen was in the next town over. It was the only place within decent distance that had any kind of nightlife. Or any place I wanted my woman hanging out anyway. Her girls were there when we pulled up and the screaming started as soon as she got in the middle of them.

We herded them all inside and got the waitress to put some tables together in the back in view of the dance floor. My woman had already warned me that she planned to dance her ass off. I was cool as long as she had a good time we were good. Her girls were a rowdy bunch, nothing at all like I expected from this bunch of debutantes shit. They started doing shots right off the bat and the boys and I decided we'd better stick to beer and nurse them shits. This bunch might be trouble.

232 | JORDAN SILVER

There was one in particular that I
knew could set shit off with one of my
brothers, then again except for Candy
who we all knew I saw a few that
might be trouble. We pretty much set
up as security and watched them do
their thing.

"I see trouble written all over this
shit?" Zak tipped his beer and rocked
back in his chair. There were a few
unknowns checking out the girls as
they danced and laughed together.
Dani had invited what looked like
every female from Briarwood and
these chicks weren't just any run of the
mill females. These were the type of
women that went the extra mile, which
meant they were all put together. Some
of them I'd never seen before but the
few I did know, huh.

We kept them supplied with
drinks and kept an eye on them to
make sure no assholes got stupid. The
women didn't seem interested in the
looks coming their way so that was our
cue to step in if anything went south. If

they were interested in dancing that was their business but the men seemed to think they were all spoken for so we were able to relax after an hour or so.

Shit she brought Gabriella Danforth over to introduce her. I kept my eyes on Logan when she rose up on her toes to kiss my cheek and offer congratulations. I could see him grinding his molars and his face drew tight. Damn not even his brother who was here to celebrate his engagement was safe.

"Thanks Gabby." I set her away from me to avert any shit and watched as the two girls walked away back to their friends on the dance floor. I looked around at the others to see if they'd noticed what I saw. I shouldn't have doubted, nosy fucks. I wasn't going to be the one to bring that shit up. Logan can be a little touchy about that subject. We all know he has the hots for the little blonde but he refused to go there. Kinda like me with Danielle. If she wanted him though his ass was in deep shit. Again I won't be the one to tell him that shit.

When some dude took her hand and led her off to dance I knew there was going to be trouble. Seven chairs scraped against the hardwood floor, one louder than the others. Jackets were discarded just in case as we moved out behind Logan but stayed back to see what play he was about to make.

Logan reached them in a few short steps and without uttering a word took her hand off the guy's shoulder and pulled her away. I know it's not the time but that shit was funny as hell. His face looked like thunder as he dragged the poor girl off the dance floor.

"Hey." She mouthed off at him but he didn't say a word to her just kept going. The guy didn't say anything just shrugged his shoulders and moved onto the next dance partner

who seemed willing and the rest of us
headed back to the table.

Logan sat her in the chair next to
his but he was still not saying
anything. She turned to me as I sat to
the other side of her.
"What's wrong with your brother?" I
tried not to smile at this shit.
"Which one?"

"The asshole jerk." She pointed
her thumb at Logan.
"Watch your damn mouth."
She turned to him and leaned in closer.
"Make me."
Oh shit. The others were glued to the
action; this shit was better than the
movies. Logan the lone wolf had met
his fucking match.

"Watch yourself little girl before
you bite off more than you can chew."
She tried getting up but he blocked her
in with his leg. "Sit your ass down,
you try getting up again you're in
trouble."

236 | JORDAN SILVER

She huffed at him but sat still shooting
daggers at him with her eyes, arms
folded like she was ready to blast his
ass.

"Well then looks like another one
bite the dust. You fuckers are falling
faster than a Red Baron bomber.
"Shut the fuck up Ty." I kicked his
chair and the ass just laughed at me. I
eyed the rest of them trying to send
them the message that maybe we
should leave and let these two deal
with their shit but the nosy fucks
weren't budging.

I went and got my girl to dance.
"You having fun baby?" I pulled her in
close for a kiss with my hands on her
ass.
"Yes it's the best, thanks for this, the
girls are having a blast. You do know
some of them have their eye on your
brothers right?"
"You playing matchmaker baby?"

She grinned up at me. "I just want everyone to be as happy as we are. And Connor, I finally get it."
"What do you get baby?" I looked into her eyes as we stopped moving in the middle of the dance floor. She's so fucking gorgeous damn. I lucked the fuck out big time.
"I understand why you were so mad. I thought I was just doing something innocent, my intentions were good but you'd already warned me not to have any contact with…him so regardless I shouldn't have met with him."

"That's absolutely right baby." I kissed her again to show her that I appreciated that shit.
"But I might forget and mess up again."
"No you won't babe because next time your ass will pay the price." She gulped and put her head on my chest. Now all was right with my world.

Chapter 15

Logan caught my eye a bit later
and gave the sign that he was leaving.
The two of them left together hand in
hand, well now. I grinned at my
brothers who were all sitting at the
table while I slow danced with my girl.
They were starting to look a little
nervous; especially Ty whose wanna
be wifey was in the crowd.

We danced two more songs
before she realized one of her girls was
missing. "Connor I don't see Gaby
anywhere."
"She left with Logan."
"She… I better go make sure she's
okay." She tried pulling out of my
arms but I held tight.

"Nope, you're not going
anywhere babe they're grown."
Speaking of which I felt like sneaking
away myself, there was a nice little
walk down to the water at the back of
this place. I nodded to my boys and

took her hand and headed out the door. Her girls were busy having fun and the guys were keeping an eye on them.

"Where are we going?" I didn't answer her, just led her through the balmy night with her hand held securely in mine. I made sure no one else had the same idea as I led her down the small incline and found a nice spot in a little copse of trees.

"Strip." I threw my jacket down on the sand so her ass wouldn't get all gritty and shit. And opened up my jeans while she kicked off her shoes and pulled her pants down her legs. The moonlight made her skin glow and the warm breeze carried her scent.

"That's good babe." I pulled her to me and kissed her with all the hunger I had inside for her. I pressed my already leaking cock into her middle. "Feel what you do to me." Her fingers in my hair pulled harder as we tongue fucked each other's mouths.

"I want to take you from behind out here in the open. I don't wanna fuck or make love sweetheart. Tonight I need to mate. This." I held up the hand with the ring. "This calls for a mating."

I got her down on her knees and spread her pink pussy lips open for my mouth. I drank from her before sinking my tongue inside. There was a heightened sense of intensity brought on by being out in the open like this. Just the moon and the stars for light as she knelt before me naked. I'd only shed my jacket and shirt, my jeans were unzipped and riding my hips; that too made a picture.

When she came on my tongue and her cries rang out in the night I moved around in front of her. I wanted her mouth before I took her. I wanted my cock to be at its fullest for this. She licked around my cockhead before taking me into her mouth and sucking. I wasn't too careful with her hair when I grabbed two fistfuls and pulled her head on and off my cock. when I started hitting he back of her throat I pulled out and got back in position behind her.

Sinking two fingers deep I went after her g-spot until she was fucking back hard against my hand.
"Please Connor."
"What do you need baby?"

"You, inside me. I need you." Her pussy clenched around my fingers as her juices flowed once more. I pulled them out and reached around feeding them to her as I slammed into her pussy. I kept the fingers in her mouth as she sucked hard and bit into her neck while jack hammering into her pussy. She never stopped screaming around my hand and cumming on my cock. I wanted to fuck her all night just like this. Never wanted it to end.

After that night we went back to being us, only with the added bonus of me loving my girl even more. Something about putting your ring on your woman's finger makes a man feel settled. And the way she flitted around the house all happy and shit, singing and dancing. That shit made my fucking life complete. On top of all that the sex was plentiful and hot as fuck. I hope that shit about women losing interest after marriage was a myth. The fuck am I saying? I'll never let that shit happen. I can't see not being inside her every chance I get just like I am now.

We had a new addition most nights at the house; it seems Logan had put Gabriella on lock down. She didn't seem too torn up about it. Though she seemed to be giving poor Logan a run for his money. It was fun to watch him trying to bring her to heel and her kicking and screaming all the way.

Most evenings their posse was over at the house going over wedding plans and bitching because I wanted shit done in weeks instead of months. Complaining asses. That was good though because it freed me up to do my thing with my brothers at night. It also had the added benefit of making the others run for cover. No one wanted to get too close to my house in the evenings when the women were coming over. They seemed to think falling in love was some sort of contagious disease or some shit.

"I'd rather be in the trenches than your house right now bro. Those women are like armed drones, they hone in on your ass and bam. Look at poor Logan."
"Fuck off Ty, let's get this shit moving so I can be done. Gabriella wants to go see some fucked up movie." He grumbled that last bit but we heard and laughed our asses off.

Gabriella is about my Dani's height, which means she's a little bit of a thing. Blonde and blue, she's a southern belle to the tips of her toes. Somewhere along the line she got a healthy dose of attitude and fuck if it isn't amusing to watch. I don't think Logan prayed this much on the battlefield. These days he's always searching the heavens for guidance. At least that's what we think he's doing when he's looking up to the sky and mumbling shit.

We'd finally got somewhere with the cigarette butts we'd found. A little undercover snooping garnered us the information that there was one particular guy who special ordered that brand of cigarette so that pretty much narrowed it down for us. We were being careful with it though until we knew all the players. It wouldn't do to show our hands too soon by going after this guy when we knew there had to be others involved.

Dennis Crampton didn't look like the kind of character to be caught up in this shit. On paper he reads like the poster boy for the senate. A farther dig into his background showed he had connections in very high places, which might make shit more difficult. But we weren't too worried about that shit. If he's dirty we'll take his ass down no question.

He's early forties with a wife and two kids. His business looked to be doing well and his finances were solid.

It was all too neat on the surface though, which sent up red flags if you knew what you were looking for. The clean in and out of his finances were just too fucking perfect.

"Find the money Quinn. We tug on that thread who knows where it will lead."

"I'm on it Logan. Con you say Danielle knows him right?"

"Yeah his wife is on the board of the charity or something like that. I asked her that shit in a roundabout way so as not to raise any suspicions. Plus I needed to know how close she was to this asshole. She doesn't have too many dealings with him but they've attended the same functions and parties. I have to figure out how to keep her away from him until we know how much of an asshole this jerk is without tipping her nosy ass off to what we're doing here."

"Even more reason to move on this shit. We might as well look into all the moneyed men in the area. Chances are if one of them is into this shit more might be as well." Logan looked at me then. I guess he was thinking of my soon to be father in law, which would be all kinds a fucked if he was involved. But I didn't get that vibe from him any of the times we'd met. Yes Dani was now in the habit of dragging me to her parents' house for dinner at least once a week.

I've learned something in the last six weeks or so since our engagement. Even a strong man has no will against the woman he loves. As long as she was happy I found myself agreeing to shit that I never thought I'd do. I gave a fuck that my brothers laughed their asses off when she dragged me off shopping or some equally female bullshit. And don't get me started on when her and Gabriella got shit into their heads about doubling up.

It usually involved some girly shit like cake testing or some crap. Thankfully I didn't have to bear that injustice alone as Gaby insisted that Lo come with. The first time he'd asked her why the fuck he had to even be involved and she'd said it was practice for their own wedding he'd turned white as a sheet. Funny shit.

Now we're over run by women
and our peace and serenity was a thing
of the past. "You got Gaby's tag yet?"
I'd put Danielle's in a matching
bracelet I'd got for us. Hers had my
initials and mine had hers. What she
didn't know was that the clasp, which
couldn't be opened without a jeweler's
help hid a tracking device. What she
didn't know wouldn't hurt her. I slept
better at night knowing that shit was
there.

"Yep she's all giddy with her
new bracelet which she's been warned
not to remove under threat of a
whipping."
"Bro they can't come off, didn't you
do what I told you?"
"Yes but we're talking about Gabriella
here. I think you got the nice one on
this deal."
"What's the matter Lo? The little
woman giving you trouble? You two
know you have to represent right? And

not make the rest of us look like assholes."

"Speaking of which Zak you're all coming to dinner tomorrow night no excuses. The girls are cooking up a feast or some shit."
"Why it's not Thanksgiving or some shit. This another one of Dani's sneak attacks?"
"I don't know Ty all I know is that when I was leaving the house she told me to pass that shit on." The grumbling and bullshit started but I knew they would be there. They didn't like disappointing her any more than I did.

Chapter 16

That night Quinn called when I was just about to fuck Dani for the second time. We were both panting and out of breath; she was sprawled across my chest barely moving but her scent still had me rock hard and seconds were sounding and looking good.

"What's up?" I ran my hand over her ass trying to dip low enough to get a finger inside her from this angle.
"We've got a problem bro. Meet at Logan's in ten."
What the fuck? I looked at the phone and hung up. "Gotta make a run babe be right back." I sucked her tongue long and hard, gave the pussy a little finger action while she grabbed my dick and then hopped into the shower for a quick wash-up.

Everyone was there by the time I arrived. No one was bleeding so whatever this was couldn't be too bad I hope.

Quinn threw an envelope across the table at me before I even sat down. Opening it I didn't understand what I was looking at at first until I saw one of the names on the sheet.

"What the fuck is this?" I jumped up from my seat ready to lay a motherfucker out.

"Calm down brother we know it's not what it looks like but we've got to figure it out." I paced the room back and forth like a caged animal after Logan said that shit. My mind was going in ten different directions at once but I couldn't grab hold of any one thought.

"There's no way her mom or dad did this so who the fuck could it be?"

"That's what we've got to find out and fast. Did you see the dates on that? They're expecting something in a week. Now Logan finally got eyes down there but they're not enough to cover the whole area the place just isn't set up for that kind of surveillance but at least we can see who's going and who's coming. The first thing we've got to do is get her to move it."

"What the fuck bro! Who the fuck are these people? She moves it they know she's onto them and they come after her. Only we can't protect her because we don't know who the fuck they are."

"There's one way to find out." Logan stood from his chair and cracked his knuckles. The others got up as well and I exhaled. My night had just gone to shit fast.

"We go after this guy now we may never know all who's involved." Devon pulled on his leather. "He'll talk, if he wants to live he'll fucking talk." I pulled my phone to call her and let her know something had come up. No doubt she'd hear the bikes revving up and wonder.

254 | JORDAN SILVER

"Babe something came up I'll be a little longer than I thought. Do me a favor and lock up and set the alarm."

"Connor is everything okay?"

"Everything's fine babe just go to sleep if I'm not back and I'll wake you when I get in. I love you."

"I love you too." I rolled my eyes at the assholes who were in my fucking face like we didn't have some serious shit to take care of.

Blue Fin was a fucking ghost town this time of night, then again so was Briarwood but at least we had a few street lights. This place for all its high-ticket homes seemed more rural. The homes were more widely spaced apart and there were more open spaces. We'd put in the GPS to where we were headed and stopped about a few hundred feet away to prepare.

"How're we doing this bro? It's your woman your call; the wife and kids are in there."
"We do it without the kids knowing we were even there. The wife goes to sleep, that's all you sleeper." Devon was good at dosing people so they didn't even know they'd been zapped. The shit you learn in the military.

"Con try not to kill this fuck before we get all the information we need."
"I just want to know how he got her info to set her up for the fall. I have my suspicions but if that shit is right

somebody just might die tonight after all."

The security on the place was a joke, or maybe that's because we knew what the fuck we were doing. There isn't any place really that Cord the sneak can't get into. We each have our own talents. Mine aren't that useful in the real world unless a motherfucker needed to get dead. And since these assholes had chosen my woman's name and information to use for their money laundering bullshit it looked like I might have to go into service.

Cord split off from Zak and Quinn who went to make sure the kids were in bed where they were supposed to be. None of us were too jazzed about putting kids out. Neither did we want to scare them half to death if they woke up in the middle of the night to seven strange men in their home. Logan and Ty went to wire the place and I waited.

Cord came back with the okay and we gave it another minute before I headed up to the room to see one Dennis Crampton. I pulled the pillow out from under his head and dropped it over his face. When his struggles lessened and he was at the edge of darkness I removed it and pulled him from the bed. Now he knows I mean fucking business and won't think twice about offing his ass.

Downstairs the others were waiting for us. I dropped him in the middle of the circle and waited for him to stop gasping for air. I'm sure we made a sight. The room was in darkness but the moonlight coming through the windows was most likely catching on the combat paint beneath our eyes and the bottom half of our faces. We'd decided that this was the best way to keep our identities hidden for now until we knew what else we were dealing with.

"Tell us about your little operation Crampton."
"I don't know what you're talking about." I think he didn't realize his finger had been broken until the loud snap sounded in the room. The shock of the pain kept him from feeling it for at least a second or two. The gag stuffed into his mouth ensured that the screams wouldn't wake his kids.

"Each time you bullshit me I'll break something else, then we'll head upstairs and get started on the others your choice."

He started pleading for his life and the lives of his family but it all fell on deaf ears. Of course next was the sob story of how he got caught up in something he had no control over. He didn't know the men who'd approached him were into smuggling. He'd tried to get out when he realized but they'd threatened his family. Fucking liar. The money Quinn had found painted a different story. He got a little tight lipped when it came to names but one more finger here or there was soon enough to loosen his fucking tongue.

I was waiting for one name. I don't know how I was so sure that it was the one I suspected. Maybe it was wishful thinking on my part. Maybe it was just me looking for any excuse to bury the fuck because he was the only one other than me to have laid hands on my woman. Don't ask my why the fuck that bothers me it just does. Still it wasn't reason enough to off a motherfucker. This shit might be though.

"So you've been smuggling drugs in and laundering money out for the past two years and no one got wind of it."

"We were always careful I was just the go between kind of."

"Kill the bullshit, we've seen the paper trial you're up to your eyeballs in this shit. Now what we want to know is how does the Dupre foundation play into all this?"

"How do you know about that?"

"I'm asking the questions here asshole. Now talk."

"They don't, that's Rob's thing. Some chick he's fucking…" I punched him before he could get the words out of his mouth. I felt hands on me pulling me back as I swung again.

"Easy brother easy." Logan whispered in my ear and reminded my ass that if I went off because he'd mentioned Dani that it would be a dead giveaway. I shook him off and shook the blood from my eye as I went to stand over the piece a shit again.

"How did he get her information?"

"What do you mean? She gave it to him she's part of the organization. She handles the money that's her thing."

No fucking way. I didn't even stumble back from the force of his words because there was no way my Dani was involved in this shit.

"You're lying, he did it himself, stole the information or tricked her somehow. How did he do it? And don't fucking lie to me again."

"I'm not lying I swear." He cowered away from me almost in the fetal position. "Why don't you go to their condo and ask them yourselves?"

"Come again?"

"Rob and his chick Karen they have a place not too far from here." Shit I didn't even know the asshole lived here I always thought he lived in Briarwood. I looked at each of my brothers in turn. Who the fuck was Karen? I'd pretty much met all of

Danielle's friends by now and I don't recall a Karen in the bunch.

"Who else is involved in this thing? Who's your boss?"
He dropped a few names that none of us knew but we could easily verify. We'd got pretty much everything we needed from him. It was time to move on to the next player.

"We'll be watching your house, you tip these guys off that we're onto them you won't draw another breath. If I find out what you're saying is a lie same goes." He clutched his maimed hand and tried to stand as we headed out the door. I wondered how he planned to explain his misfortune to his wife and kids.

Chapter 17

On a hunch I called up Dani on the way back to our bikes. She sounded like she'd already been fast asleep which just might work in my favor. She wasn't exactly with it when she first woke up. "Babe does Karen still work for you guys?" "Connor? Yes. What, what happened?"

"Nothing happened baby just go back to sleep." She mumbled something and hung up. I shut the phone off and turned to the others. "At least that answers that question." I didn't even have to say anything else. Tyler got out his nifty little reconfigured smartphone and put in some info.

By the time we reached the bikes he had what he was looking for. "Got her. Karen Skeet twenty-eight. Huh looks like the asshole traded way the fuck down. He held up the screen to show us the bleached blonde who looked a little rough around the edges.

"What does it say Ty?" I climbed on the back of my ride and waited while the others did the same. I was already pissed way the fuck off so whatever he found out about this bitch won't make much of a difference but I liked to have as much information as possible when I was about to do a job.

I wouldn't like to find out after the fact for instance that this person was being used against her will or some shit. Or that they were holding a gun to her sick mother's head or some sick shit like that and she had no other choice. That shit isn't just for the movies. There are some seriously fucked up individuals who makes Hollywood look like child's play.

"She's a finance major from Vassar. Coulda fooled me, maybe this is an old picture or some shit. Says here she's been working for the charity for the past year and a half give or take."

"Huh, Dani says she ran into that asshole about a year or so ago. So how did they play it? Did he send Karen in or did he meet her and got the idea. Nah, Crampton said they'd been smuggling for two years. I'm more inclined to believe he sent her in for this purpose. Is there anyway to tell if she's really who she says she is?"

"On it." We had to wait a little longer for his tool to do its thing. "Nope the real Karen Skeet lives in Greensborough and is married with a young child. The date of birth and credentials are the same and since this one isn't using her Ivy-league education to steal I'm more inclined to believe that she's the real thing."
This Karen was a brunette who looked like a professional as opposed to a recovering alcoholic.

"Let's go I've got the addy." I did a Google earth search and

266 | JORDAN SILVER

pinpointed the asshole's location. It
was a condo so there was more traffic
around him than the last one but
nothing we couldn't get around. This
area was more yuppie central for the
younger crowd. There were six condos
three and three on a little cul de sac.

The lights were off here as well.
Everyone was asleep granted they
were even home. There was no real
way of telling unless we called and I
didn't want to do that. I liked having
the element of surprise on my side.

"You guys don't even need to
come in with me. In and out in five."
"No way bro you're not killing him."
"Why the fuck not Logan?"

"Use your head Connor. The
wrong person go digging and uncover
the shit they're up to with your
woman's name all over this shit and it
leads back to you they'll have your ass
pegged in ten seconds flat."

"No problem I already reversed
the trail, it leads right back to her."

Quinn grinned like the fucking grim reaper. He's another murdering fuck, which is just what I needed on my side right now.

"I don't see why I can't just break both their fucking necks right now and be done with it."
"Because we're not animals. Besides I've got a better idea. When we move the money the men coming in a week will do our dirty work for us. We're here so you can get this shit out of your system but you're not killing them."

Well fuck. We didn't have to neutralize the neighbors on either side. Just cut out the lock on the backdoor to the place and slip inside. We headed up the stairs like smoke and did the same to his door. Inside the others didn't actually hang back but they let me take the lead.

I found them in bed asleep, didn't look like there was any love lost between these two or maybe that's

how people usually slept. The fuck I
know. I haven't slept without some
part of me touching Danielle since I
brought her home. Not the time
Connor.

I wasn't quiet as I made my way
around to his side of the bed. Chump
had his woman closest to the door right
in the line of fire. I started beating his
ass before I'd dragged him completely
out of bed. Logan was there to shush
her with a hand around her throat when
she woke up startled. With the shit
these two were into you'd think they'd
sleep with one eye open. I guess it's
true what they say. Only the guilty can
sleep the sleep of the dead after the
shit they've done.

"Who are you?" He had got one
question in before I threw his ass into
the wall.
"Tell me this, did you go after her to
fuck her life over huh?" Either he
recognized my voice from the one time
we'd met or he was one cognizant
motherfucker when he woke up

because his eyes widened in understanding.

"I didn't. Stop what're you doing?" Is he stupid what the fuck did it look like I was doing?
"I'll tell you what I'm doing. I'm going to beat you to within an inch of your life for fucking with what's mine. Then I'm gonna leave you to your smuggler friends to finish you the fuck off." Yeah maybe Logan had the right idea there after all.

The others were tossing the place while I did my thing. I guess they were looking for any information they could use that we hadn't found at Crampton's. I wasn't too interested in that shit right now. I wanted to obliterate this fucker and his partner in crime. I could hear Logan whispering to her in the background while I plowed my fist into Robert's face. When I was sure he wasn't going to be able to see out of his eyes anytime soon I started on his body.

He'd stopped begging me for his life about five minutes ago when I'd broken his fucking nose. I imagine he was in immense pain from me pulverizing his internal organs. I concentrated mostly on the kidneys. Logan said I couldn't kill him right now he didn't say anything about him dying at some later date from his injuries.

I used all my training to attack only the areas that would do the most damage. It was dispassionate and precise. He was unconscious by the time I realized my hands were tired as fuck. I left him on the floor in a heap and walked over to where Logan still had her. Grabbing her by the throat I pulled her out of his hands.

"What's your real name?" She was shaking like a leaf.
"I already got that info bro let's be out."

"Was she nice to you? I bet she treated you better than anyone ever has in your pathetic life but you were willing to fuck her over. I ought to kill your ass right now." She made a sound of distress as her eyes flew to the bloody mess on the floor and then back to mine. I had to satisfy myself with a hard slap across her face that hopefully loosened a few teeth before Logan was hustling me out of the room.

By the time we got back to the compound my woman was fast asleep so I was able to slip into the shower and wash off most of the evidence. Wasn't shit I could do about my bruised knuckles though so I just doctored them and climbed into bed.

"Connor?" She sighed and turned to me in her sleep. I should probably leave her alone but I needed her. It fucked with my head that while I'd thought I was protecting her something like that was going on behind the scenes. Something that could have potentially taken her away from me. I don't understand that shit as well as Quinn does but from what little I'd seen they'd had her tied up nice and tight with a little bow for anyone who came looking.

I ran my hands over her slowly, softly, gentling her awake with my mouth on hers. She sighed into my mouth and opened up for my tongue. I kissed my way down her middle until I reached her heat. She'd taken a bath after I'd left. Her fresh flowery scent was almost as intoxicating as the scent of her pussy when I'd just fucked her. I preferred her a little dirty though so I got to work making her so.

She moved against my mouth as I tongue fucked her into full wakefulness. Her hands came down to play in my hair as I lifted her to my mouth so I could sink my tongue deeper. When she was swollen and hot around my tongue I eased up her body and pulling her head back so I could see into her eyes I slipped into her. I closed my eyes against the enormity of the feelings that hit me as I started fucking into her body nice and slow.

Folding her close I rocked our bodies in a slow dance of love, whispering words of love and praise in her ears as her body strained up to meet mine. Lifting one of her legs higher on my hip I went in deeper but still kept the slow glide in and out of her until we both came with a groan.

I fitted her body next to mine after pulling out minutes later. "Sleep baby." She was out in seconds.

Epilogue

"What's up brother?" We were all gathered in Logan's kitchen because he'd called and said we needed a sit down. Usually that meant serious business. I was in a hurry to get back to my woman because she'd been acting kind of frisky before the phone rang. And that teasing whisper in my ear just before the phone rang had given me ideas.

I'd almost brushed Logan off but that was something none of us had ever done. Our code was such that when one sent out an S.O.S we all answered no matter what. We'd learned in our time together to put each other first, to always have each other's backs. That's how we'd made it through some of the toughest runs in our careers. That kind of trust was not to be tampered with. I'm pretty sure we'd all be old and grey and still living by that code. But the last time these fuckers called me out of my bed I'd

276 | JORDAN SILVER

had to lie to my woman about how my knuckles got fucked up.

"I got a call from the C.O." The room fell silent. We were out yes but we all knew because of our team's special skills we would never truly be free. They'd built the team yes, but we'd made it what it was and what it was was an elite force of manpower equaled to none.

"I'm not going. Whatever it is, wherever it is, I'm done." Tyler stormed out of the kitchen as the rest of us looked on. We knew why he felt this way the sentiment I'm sure was shared by most if not all of us; but we also knew no matter what gripes we might have that it wasn't that easy to turn our backs on our calling.

"Go after him Connor." Logan ordered me while the others stayed silent. No one wanted to tangle with Ty when he got like this. He could be a hardheaded fuck when his blood was up about something. "Why do I always get sent to the tiger's lair?" It's true whenever he acts up they all look to me to rein him in, I've got the battle scars to prove it.

I didn't have time to consider the ramifications of what Logan's announcement meant for me. Whatever it is if he hadn't told them to go fuck themselves then it must be bad. "Because you two are more alike in that aspect and you're the only one who can reach him, go get him brother before he hurts something." I left the room and my brothers to go face a man's anger.

He was kicking the wheel of his bike when I came out. "Save it Con I'm not doing it, not this time, fuck them." I let him work off some of the steam he had working there knowing that it was only after he'd gotten most of it out of his system that he'd be able to hear me. It was always this way with Ty. He could get hot at the drop of a hat. I'd once seen him destroy a whole room in less than ten minutes

278 | JORDAN SILVER

and there'd been no way to stop him. But when the blood was no longer in his eyes and he calmed down a little he was as quiet as a lamb. It was freaky to see. "What's destroying your bike gonna prove brother?" He glared at me before walking off.

"I don't owe those lying fucks anything. I gave them my youth and the best part of me and for what? So some over inflated windbag could sit behind a desk and make money on the backs of our brothers and sisters in arms? And now they want to cut their benefits and shit but they need our help? Fuck that shit, how about I go take their asses out? They're the real enemy the fucks."

What could I say to that? We all agreed, it was fucked what was going on. Most people had no idea how under appreciated the men and women who fought for their freedoms really were. They didn't know the sacrifices that were made each and everyday. But we did it because we believed in something, because that code of honor ran deep. Deep enough to overlook the mishandling of funds and the stench of corruption, that was even now kept well hidden from the public. But now wasn't the time to go there either.

"It's not for them brother, whatever this is you know it's got to be some fucked up shit for Logan to even contemplate dragging us back in. We knew when we left there was a possibility that it was only a matter of time before they came looking. Well it's happening sooner than we thought but hey."

He kicked at the weeds that had started growing in Logan's back yard. We're gonna have to make a run soon with the lawnmower. "I refuse to put anymore into this shit. They've taken all they're gonna get. What's the point of us over there fighting this shit while they're making backroom deals with the same fucks we're trying to eliminate?" Shit this was going to be harder than I thought. Firstly because I agreed with him one hundred percent and secondly I didn't really want to leave my woman and go anywhere either. This whole thing was fucked already and we hadn't even left stateside.

"Ty, you know that if this thing wasn't important whatever it is, Logan wouldn't have brought it to the table. You also know that if one goes we all go so there's no point in fighting it. Let's just see what Logan has to say. We all know that the fucks in office are assholes but this is not about them. Chances are this is some shit that can fuck with our citizens and we took the oath brother. God, family, country, hanging up our weapons didn't change that. We are what we are and you can't tell me as mad as you are right now that you're willing to leave our people in a vulnerable position whether from domestic or foreign fuck ups." I knew I was getting through to him when he finally stopped his mad pacing and just stared off into the distance. "Fuck."

I followed him back inside with a slap on the back. The danger wasn't exactly over but at least he was willing to listen to reason. The others were standing around waiting. I know they wouldn't have carried on without us, that is not our way. When you've spent as much time together in the kind of situations we have you get to know each other pretty damn well. I know my brothers and they know me, and that's why I knew that none of them were too happy with this turn of events.

"Before we go any farther, we've got a problem; Connor." I knew what he meant, I was barely holding onto my sanity by a thread. This was the reason we'd all made a pact, the saying goes never leave a man behind. For us that went double, it was fucked to be in the heat of combat with your woman thousands of miles away. It was fucked not knowing every second of everyday if she needed you.

As men we do what we have to, that doesn't make that shit easy. That's why we'd agreed to a man that we wouldn't get hitched before our gig was up. If it had happened, if one of us had fallen in love before now we would've played the hand we were dealt. But luck and prayer was on our side because for the fourteen years that each of us were in, we never felt that pull.

Now though, my ass was in the sling and so was Logan's. How was I going to leave her? I'm honor and duty bound to answer the call there's no two ways about it. Retired or not, my skills were honed in this man's navy, he made me what I am for a reason. I pretty much know they think they own my ass for a lifetime. I'll let them think that until I snap that cord, until then I have to do what I must for my countrymen and women. But how can I leave her?

"Let's hear what they want first then I'll decide if it's worth leaving my woman here unprotected." Zak and Quinn nodded in agreement as we all pulled up a seat. All except Ty who was once again pacing back and forth like a caged beast. As opposed to leaving our women behind as the rest of us were, Ty was the worst. His history made sure of that but that's his story to tell.

"Khalid has surfaced." Everyone in the room tensed. Son of a mother-fucking bitch.

"Where, when?" I was almost at the edge of my seat. This fuck is one of the deadliest assholes to ever walk the earth. The Desert Fox, that's what we'd tagged him. Early on in our career we'd been given Intel but just before we'd been set to smoke him out of his hole in Kabul he'd disappeared.

Since then he'd been attributed the blame for more terrorist acts than any man before him, but always he stayed in the shadows. No one knew where he was or who was hiding him, but it stood to reason that he must have friends in very high places. There was no way for such a well known wanted man to have stayed so well hidden all these years without the help of some very influential and powerful people.

"The Sudan."

Fuck I knew there was no way we were gonna pass this shit up. The chance to bring down the world's leading terrorist. He'd evaded us, and the others who'd come before us for all these years. The only one we'd missed though we were only in on the tail end of that deal.

By the time our team had formed they'd already moved onto the new kid on the block. There had been some assholes on a par with the Fox but none could ever quite take his place. My mind was already on the fact that I had to leave her. Logan had a hard on for Khalid, he hated the fuck with a vengeance. Ever since he'd blown up a school of young girls just before

Logan had been able to reach them and lead them out to safety. That was maybe ten years ago but Logan hadn't forgotten. But could he leave Gaby?

"I'm in." Zak threw his hat in the ring first and so it went. Fuck, Danielle. My gut tied itself in knots at the thought of leaving her now when everything was still so new. We'd only just dealt with her ex and his bullshit. She still didn't know anything about that shit. The woman who we'd learned days later was really one Rosalind Haynes from Louisiana had given her some bullshit story about a family emergency back home. True to form my girl had offered her help in anyway necessary but I was there to smooth that shit over.

Haven't seen hide nor hair of Robert in the last few days and it was only a day or so before the ship was due to dock. Now with this shit there was just too much going on at once. My first inclination is to say fuck no. I don't want to leave her here with this shit so up in the air.

"When do we have to give them an answer and how soon will we have to be in the desert?" I broke off when Ty started his shit again.

" We said we'd never do that shit, and this is fucked Logan that you'd even think of dong it. You and Connor have your women now you can't just up and leave them no matter what the fuck. They come first fuck everything else. Fuck these assholes. Fourteen fucking years, I gave them fourteen years of my life and would've given them the whole twenty, and for what? So they can lie to our fucking faces like we're fucking sheep." Tyler bunched his fists as he prowled around the room.

"We're not doing this for them brother, you know this. They're protected, you better believe their asses are covered. We're doing this for each other and for the men and women we pass everyday on the streets. Because we all know they'd sell us out to the highest bidder. As for the girls, you think this is easy for me? I don't even let Danielle drive herself to fucking work and with this smuggling shit and the money moved where they can't find it it's fucked." I had to stop talking because I was only talking myself out of going.

"I'm telling you right now Logan if I find out this is some fucked up bullshit to have us protecting their oil interest or diamond mines or some shit I'm going to put a bullet in some fuck's head."
"I thought you calmed him down Connor?" I shrugged my shoulders at Quinn.
"Hey this is his calm."

"I haven't given them an answer as yet but most likely if we answer the call it will be in a few weeks at the least."

I went home a lot later than expected so I knew she would be asleep by now. I just needed to feel her under my hands. In the next few days I was going to have to get my fill of her, enough to carry me through the weeks ahead.

Fuck, we hadn't had enough time. How could I leave her now when it was all still so new? What kind of warrior will I be? Will I be able to focus or would my mind be back here with her? Will I make unnecessary mistakes? These thoughts and more played through my head as I made my way upstairs to our bedroom.

I stripped as soon as I hit the bedroom door without turning on the light and made my way over to the bed. She'd fallen asleep reading so I removed her reading tablet that was lying on her chest and placed it on the night table before pulling her into my arms. "Connor." Her voice was sleep soft and sexy as she snuggled into m.

"Yeah baby wake up I need you." Her hand made a sleepy foray into my hair as she searched for my mouth with hers. She was naked the way I like her to be when we sleep and I ran my hands over her. Pulling my mouth away I latched onto her nipple and sucked it into my mouth while running my finger down her middle until I reached her pussy. Slipping three fingers inside her I went back to her mouth as she fucked herself on my fingers. "Connor?" her voice sounded unsure as my mouth became ravenous on hers and my fingers plunged deeper and deeper. All I could think about was leaving her, being away from her for all those weeks or months or however the fuck long this cluster fuck takes.

"Get on your knees and whatever I do don't be afraid." I helped her into position and lined up behind her. Her pussy was already wet and swollen from my fingers as I moved my mouth over her. I swiped her with my tongue back and forth while holding her hips in place before sinking my tongue inside. She screamed and grabbed onto the sheets while I ate her, trying to get her taste to stay with me. When I'd made her cum in my mouth I knelt behind her and slipped my cock home. I went in hard and deep on my first thrust. I was pissed the fuck off and fair or not I intended on taking out that frustration on her sweet little pussy tonight. That's why the warning before the fuck. "Hold on."

When she looked over her shoulder in surprise I knew I was doing some shit she'd never experienced at my hands before but still I didn't let up. I couldn't; I was at a place in my head that I'd never been. The thought of having to leave her behind and go into uncertain danger fucked with my head and my heart. If I could take part of her with me I would. For now all I will have are memories.

"I want to look at you baby." I pulled out and helped her onto her back before sliding back into her gently. I looked into her eyes as I loved her. Trying to imprint her beauty on my brain.

"What is it Connor?" Her hand came up to caress my cheek as I shook my head at her. Not yet, let me enjoy this before I shatter us both with the shit I was about to do to her. I'd promised her that I'd never leave her. As much as I was against leaving my woman behind I've come to learn that she's fucking petrified of that shit.

Now I have to break my word. I buried my face in her neck so she wouldn't see the fight going on in my soul. "My Dani. I love you so fucking much. Will you marry me tomorrow if I asked?" She nodded her head yes without question, her eyes worried because she knew something was wrong with her man.

I made slow sweet love to her for the rest of the night, turning to her throughout the night and slipping into her waiting warmth. Each time I turned to her or rolled her beneath me she was there with me. Accepting me into her sweet body without question.

At least I could do that much for her, give her my name so that the child I'm sure I'd planted inside her would have my name.

THE END

Thank you very much for reading

You may reach the author @

Jordansilver.net

amazon.com/author/jordansilver

Jordan Silver is the author of over thirty erotic romance novels available on amazon and other ebook platforms; with three in print.